40 HUMOUROUS BRITISH TRADITIONS

To Lutz & Julie:
Thank you very much
for appreciating my
book.
With best wishes,
Julian

First Published in Great Britain 2013 by Mirador Publishing

First edition: 2013

Any reference to real names and places are purely fictional and are constructs of the author. Any offence the references produce is unintentional and in no way reflects the reality of any locations or people involved.

A copy of this work is available through the British Library.

ISBN : 978-1-909220-39-3

Mirador Publishing
Mirador
Wearne Lane
Langport
Somerset
TA10 9HB

40 Humourous British Traditions

By

Julian Worker

Mirador Publishing
www.miradorpublishing.com

Table of Contents

Walking the Weasel in Cleckheaton

According to the *Lindisfarne Chronicles*, "Walking the Ways All" was an annual tradition in all Anglo-Saxon towns. The third Thursday in July was set aside for the townsfolk to walk along the common pathways and re-establish their right to frequent these paths. According to the English Common Law, if this annual reclamation wasn't performed these pathways would become the property of the local landowner, who could then collect tithes from the townsfolk for using the paths.

In 1471 a drunken clerk, Oliver de Turnhouse, misheard the Cleckheaton town crier's proclamation and so the new tradition began. The town mayor for that year, William de Gradlove, had to walk around the paths dragging a small mammal with sharp teeth behind him. Animal rights not being of top priority, it's believed that a different weasel was used every year.

One particularly cruel mayor, Edgar Stride, decided to ride around the paths on a horse as he didn't want to be bitten in the ankle by the weasel. However, his fear caused his death. The weasel's leash wasn't quite long enough for it to walk on the ground. Not wishing to be strangled, the weasel fought and writhed against the leash until it managed to sink its teeth into the horse's haunch. This powerful nip caused the horse to bolt - Stride was knocked from the horse's back when it ran under a low branch. Stride hit the ground hard and died from his injuries. His quick-thinking deputy, Mortimer Sanderson, jumped over Stride's body and managed to pick up the weasel's leash before it could effect an escape. He walked around the rest of the paths without further mishap. This act of quick-wittedness is now enshrined in the ceremony. Since that day, when the mayors approach the area known as Mortimer's Leap, they have to sprint for approximately one hundred yards, ensuring that the weasel is keeping up.

Only when the role of 'The Walking Weasel' became an officially recognized position in 1661, to commemorate the restoration of the monarchy, did the same weasel perform the ceremony more than once. Indeed, it's understood that the walk began to appeal to the weasel, as it came across the warrens of the local rabbits, which it could visit at other times of the year. The record for the number of walks undertaken by one weasel is 6 between 1872 and 1877 by Walter the weasel, whose son Barney succeeded him for a further 4 years. The ceremony has been performed nearly 540 times in a continuous line that hasn't been broken by World Wars, Civil War, or the election of Margaret Thatcher.

Dancing Around the Windmill in Somerset

The concept of the Village Idiot is a long-held tradition that was refined to its highest degree in rural Somerset in the 1300s. At that time the position of Village Idiot was an official job title and had a salary, though it was paid in acorns. Both men and women could apply for the role in the annual Dancing Around the Windmill contest, which took place in November - the windiest time of the year. The selection process involved drinking copious amounts of cider and then dancing between the sails of the windmill.

Nowadays, there is no job of Village Idiot but the contest continues in purely ceremonial form, though the rules are almost the same. The only change from 700 years ago is that the dancers don't have to wear oak clogs. Starting at 8 o'clock in the morning the contestants are presented to the watching crowds in their fool's costumes. Each contestant is given a gallon vat of apple cider, which they must drink by nine o'clock or be disqualified from the dance. They are not allowed to eat any food during this time.

At ten past eight, the potential idiots start dancing through the sails carrying their vats with them. The contest is judged by three umpires who perform various tasks. The contestants are supposed to avoid the sails by either slowing down or speeding up their dance, but they must never stop or they will be penalized a point by an umpire. Dancers must not move more than 10 feet from the windmill or they will be deducted a point. Contestants who are hit by a sail are either deducted a point if they remain conscious or disqualified if they have to be sent to the hospital by the umpire. If the umpires deduct three points from a contestant then their contest is over. The contest continues until there is only one person left who hasn't been disqualified.

Turtle Rinsing in London

It's a little known fact that every turtle that swims up the River Thames past Tower Bridge into the Pool of London becomes the property and responsibility of the monarch. This rule is part of the Common Law of England and dates back to the time of Queen Matilda in the 12th Century.

The Royal Turtle Surveyor has to be notified if a turtle reaches the Pool of London so the ceremony of Turtle Rinsing can occur. This old procedure involves the Royal Turtle Surveyor, The Royal Turtle Deputy-Surveyor, the Royal Net Bearer, The Royal Water Bagpiper, and the Master of the Hose. From the Tower of London, these five officials proceed towards the turtle in a launch bearing The Royal Standard.

Once the turtle is observed by The Royal Turtle Deputy-Surveyor using a spyglass, the Royal Net Bearer apprehends the creature in a special Turtle net that's over two hundred years old. Once clear of the water, the turtle in the net is raised to shoulder height. Using a 500-year old hose made from Staffordshire Boar hide, the Master of the Hose sprays the creature for "one round of ye reel," which is danced by the Royal Turtle Surveyor and The Royal Turtle Deputy-Surveyor. The Royal Water Bagpiper accompanies the dance.

Once the reel is complete, the rinsed turtle is returned to the water. In the past, the turtle was observed swimming vigorously for the open sea; however in recent years they have mainly hung around HMS Belfast waiting for tourists to drop food to them.

Historians believe that the Turtle Rinsing was created because of Matilda's desire to keep her supporters happy by giving them jobs in the Royal Household that were purely ceremonial in nature. Other such jobs include The Royal Wasp Counter in the Hunting Forests, The Royal Cloud Shape Describer, and the Royal Maker of Cubes from Honey.

Dry Stone Walling in Littondale

"I can build a better stone wall than you can," "My wall is straighter than yours," and "My stone wall is longer than yours" were all familiar brags in 16th Century Yorkshire when the farmers were building walls around Littondale to enclose their sheep and cows.

After 100 years of controversy and shoving between rival wall builders a man called Clarence Boycott decided to settle the issue once and for all. He began the Littondale Wall Contest in 1632, where farmers from this valley and beyond were given the task of building a wall up a hill within the 24 hours of the day of the summer solstice.

Each farmer was allowed three helpers who could bring food and drink to him and place stones along the line of the wall, but they must not help him construct the wall. The helpers could also hose down the farmer on the hotter days.

The farmer is not allowed to seek others' help in the alignment of the wall, nor is he allowed to use anyone as a marker to aim his wall at. The farmer is not allowed to plant a scarecrow on the hill, nor is he allowed to use his sheepdog in any way.

Once the 24 hours are completed then all competitors must leave the area. The walls are guarded until the judging can commence at first light - this is to prevent any sabotage of the walls by a rival.

The length of the wall isn't the main criterion for a winning wall. Above all the judges look for straightness and sturdiness in the wall; it has to be strong enough to prevent a determined sheep or bullock from escaping. Height is also an important factor as there's no point in building a wall that an animal can jump over.

The farmer also has to allow for a gate to be included in his wall though he doesn't have to put the gate in place himself. This rule was introduced when the winner of the 1763 contest, Hadrian Roman from the Scottish Borders, built a very long wall up the hillside but then pointed out to the judges that he wouldn't be able to get any sheep into the area contained by the wall as there was no gate. Hadrian commented, "it has run in my family for hundreds of years to build walls without gates, but they're of no use to either man or beast."

In 1842, Jeremiah Spalding built the longest wall in the history of the competition. It stretched 167 yards up the hill and was in a perfectly straight line. However, this wall didn't win as it was just two feet high and one foot wide – the judges didn't believe Jeremiah's excuse that he was a grass-hopper breeder.

The competitors mustn't touch any alcohol during the contest – this was after an unfortunate situation in 1802 when Barry Cockerill consumed too much cider in the summer sun and started to build his wall across the path of the other participants. This lead to a sharp exchange of words and the cancelling of the contest until the following day, so that Cockerill's wall could be dismantled.

Gabriel Herriott won the Littondale Wall contest a record five times, including an unprecedented hat-trick between 1845 and 1847. His detractors claim that Herriott used his pointer Snowball illegally by having the dog take one step uphill every five minutes, thus giving Herriott a theodolite other competitors didn't have.

The shortest wall on record measured 12 feet 8 inches in length and was built by a Master James Handysides in 1683. To be fair, James was the owner of a particularly ferocious bull, which would explain why the wall was 33 feet high.

This structure still stands today and is used as a windbreak by the local cattle in stormy weather.

Some competitors in the first years of the Littondale Wall contest didn't survive through the 24 hours. In 1647 Arthur Welland was killed when his wall collapsed on him during a severe rainstorm. In 1653 Peter Garton was bludgeoned by a local farmer when he started to dismantle the farmer's house for stone. In 1660, Gilbert Bruyle was shot by another farmer when he was discovered 'taking a break from walling' with the farmer's wife.

Animal Gambling in the Forest of Dean

Before the days of casinos and one-armed bandits in pubs, people found many different ways to gamble. They would sometimes bet on two flies crawling up a wall; if the wall was missing they'd bet on the number of raindrops falling on someone's hat in their front room or the number of leaves that blew in from the surrounding garden.

In the Forest of Dean the locals hit upon a novel method of satisfying their gambling habit – use animals in a number of games and contests.

Snail racing was a particular favourite, especially with the heavy drinkers. People would place a bet on their selected snail and then go to the pub for four hours before returning to the snail course to see the climax of the one yard race.

Another favourite was 'push the mouse.' Ten people used to play this game at the same time. A cat was placed in a box that was turned on its side, so that the cat was facing the 'push the mouse' contraption, which comprised ten sticks, one yard in length. At the end of each stick a mouse had been painted that was a different colour from the others. Contestants selected a mouse and then tried to attract the cat's attention by waving their mouse at the cat without touching it. Competitors who touched the cat with their mouse were disqualified. The winner was the person whose mouse was the first to be swatted by the cat. These contests could take many hours as some cats fell asleep and couldn't be woken by any fair means. In 1813 a short-sighted cat called Vincent pounced on the contraption itself and all bets were declared null and void.

The village cats were also used as roulette wheels. Their

beds were placed on the ground and sixteen different segments were drawn around the bed. Gamblers placed their money in the segment that they thought the cat's nose would be pointing at. The tired cat was then placed in its bed – it would then turn round and round until it found a comfortable position and one lucky gambler would win the money. Cats whose owners read books on feng shui weren't allowed to take part in this contest.

The local fish pond was the scene of more gambling. People baked their own bread using various recipes and then played "feed the fish". People threw pieces of bread into the water and the first piece of bread eaten would win its baker the prize. In 1892, after ten years of overzealous competition the fish in the pond were so large that they could barely swim and so there was a five-year hiatus before the contest recommenced.

Another contest was 'Attract the Mouse," which was played in the house of Martha Grable. She had a large mousehole in her skirting board. Gamblers placed their pieces of cheese around the hole and then crouched down behind the sofa to wait. The Cheese Judge ensured that each piece was genuine cheese and hadn't been doctored by a mouse attractant. The judge also ensured that each piece of cheese was exactly three feet from the hole. The winner was the person whose piece of cheese was first eaten by the mouse. A mouse sniffing at a piece of cheese didn't count.

The most popular contest was "Guess the spots on the ladybird." The ladybird judge would catch an insect and ask people to place bets on the number of spots. If the number of spots wasn't guessed correctly all bets were carried over into the next guess. In 1763, an apparent plague of 10-spotted ladybirds was found to be a hoax perpetrated by Andrew Craig, the local painter, who was banned from all gambling events for 200 years.

Shearing and Knitting in Llandrindod Wells

Wales has a glorious tradition of producing garments made from wool and the fur of other animals such as weasels and badgers. These animals became particularly important during the great sheep blight of the 1710s, when the wool of the sheep became unusable for clothing because the lanolin content was almost nil.

However, there were a number of problems using weasels and badgers as substitutes. The first was that weasels and badgers are wild animals and are hard to catch humanely. Secondly, they are rather attached to their coats and put up a huge fight when someone tries to shear them. Thirdly, you have to be able to knit a useable garment from the fur quickly and easily.

Out of these problems arose the Shearing and Knitting festival of Llandrindod Wells, which stretches back to 1726. The festival is held in early July so that the animals won't get too cold at night after being sheared. Indeed, in years when there's an abundance of wool replacement coats are provided for those animals that have been sheared. Walkers in this part of Wales are sometimes surprised to see weasels wearing wool socks in the undergrowth.

On the first day of the festival the Hunt the Badger and Weasel contest takes place. Teams of three roam the hills and valleys trying to catch the animals using only their bare hands. No traps, weapons, or animals may be used. Five points are awarded for each badger that's caught and three points per weasel.

The animals must be captured alive. This rule was introduced in 1872 when Ebenezer Davies was found to have stolen half the exhibits from the Natural History section of the Shrewsbury Museum with the intention of using them in the contest. Although being stuffed made them easier to shear, the judges felt that this idea went against the spirit of the contest and handed Davies over to Shropshire Police.

The record haul for animals caught was 242 points in 1907 by the Jenkins family from Port Talbot, though rumours abounded that many weasels had been brought from South Wales by other family members and accidentally dropped in the path of the Jenkins boys as they searched for animals.

The shearing takes place on the second day of the festival. Badgers make a fearful noise when being sheared, like someone drowning in their own blood, so contestants have to wear ear protectors. The winner of the badger shearing is the person who can produce the largest unbroken pelt. If even a speck of blood is seen by the judges, the shearer is disqualified.

Weasels are more difficult to shear and have very sharp teeth, so the contestants usually place a toothpick between those teeth for the animal to bite on. The scissors from a Swiss Army knife are the best implement to use for shearing weasels as they are sharp and easy to use around the delicate parts of the creature. Fur from 20 weasels can make a sweater for a small boy, making weasel fur the most expensive in the world.

The knitting on the third day is the most keenly contested part of the three days. There are many sections: the badger wool and weasel fur is divided up between the contestants, who then have to create a man's sweater in four hours using their wool or fur and combining it with sheep's wool where appropriate. Design and knitting skills are both required to win this contest. Betty Evans won 14 times between 1954 and 1997, chiefly because her designs always incorporated the words Wales, English, Now, and Leave in some order.

It's thought that her designs hit a chord with the Welsh-speaking judges from the Plaid Cymru party.

Another knitting contest was the "direct from the sheep" knitting contest where the knitters created their items directly from the animal without spinning the wool first. This involves incredible patience - knot-making skills of the highest order are required given the flimsiness of the wool. An animal psychologist is also on hand to ensure that the sheep endures no mental cruelty during the contest. It's believed that some sheep feel as though they are being unravelled and become concerned about their future.

Dyke Leaping in Lincolnshire

The sport of dyke leaping has been taking place in the Fens and Lincolnshire since the time of Hereward the Wake and his insurrection against the Norman invaders.

Many villages in the counties of Lincolnshire, Cambridgeshire and in Western Norfolk have their own festival each year to celebrate Hereward's successful evasion of the Norman invasion.

There are competitions for children, adults up to the age of 30, and for those 30 and above. Men, women, boys and girls compete in the same event – the only stipulation being that everyone must wear a brown sack in memory of Hereward's sartorial elegance.

For over 800 years people were allowed to use trees, branches and poles to help them across the dykes, but due to human rights issues the poles are no longer forced to stand up to their waists in cold water for around six hours. As a nod to the history of the event, the only alcoholic beverage available during a dyke leaping is vodka.

The idea behind the dyke leaping is that competitors are allowed to take a run up and then propel themselves across the dyke by any means possible without landing in the water. Special moisture judges are on hand with vast paper rolls to check that competitors don't touch the water as they crossed the dyke. If the judges find a damp mark then you are out of the competition. There can be any number of rounds of dyke-leaping. It should be noted that the distance that people are allowed to use as a run-up is reduced by 5 feet per round until there's only one dry competitor left.

The only trouble that's ever occurred was in 1971 when a pressure group of American lesbians held up placards denouncing the demeaning manner in which their fellow women were being treated. Only when they were shown a copy of the Oxford English Dictionary and watched the event taking place did they realize their mistake. One of the women even took part in the event – she came fifth,winning a prize of a beetroot, which she wasn't allowed to take back to the USA because of their laws prohibiting importation of foreign fruit and vegetables.

The only fatality was in 1671 when Henry de Belancourt starved to death at the King's Lynn sea-dyke leaping. He was determined to win and so decided to vault across using a small willow tree. In the final round a successful leap would have won him the first prize of six acorns, but he got stuck halfway. Unfortunately, the tide came in and because the rules forbid any outside interference Henry decided to wait – however, the tide came in for two weeks and by the tenth day Henry was delusional and believed himself to be St Simeon Stylites. He eventually passed out and was draped over the tree when rescued. Attempts made to revive him failed. His last recorded words were "acorns, acorns, where are my acorns?" Since 1671, in Henry's honour, the Squirrel Cup has been awarded to the winner of the King's Lynn sea-dyke leaping contest.

Obscene Vegetable Growing in Chillingham

Carrots, potatoes and cucumbers have often caused amusement to men who find that the shapes of these vegetables resemble parts of their own anatomy.

It's believed that the monastery at Jarrow was the first to ban these particular vegetables from their kitchen garden in the 8th Century. This was due to the Abbot's belief that all temptation must be removed from the monks' lives. He was convinced that stroking a carrot or fondling a potato could instill carnal desires in the mind of a monk, especially on a dark winter's night when they all huddled for warmth around a solitary candle.

The Abbot wrote, "it be a sin before God to stroke a carrot and think of thy brother monk in an unnatural way." Leeks, rhubarb and celery were tolerated, although they couldn't be grown any longer than two feet in length for fear of them being used in "pain or pleasure" sessions in the refectory before matins.

In the 1360s there must have been a particularly healthy crop of carrots and cucumbers as the local chronicler in Chillingham in Northumberland reported "ye multitude of faintinges and swooningges" amongst the local ladies on market days. It's believed that the obscene vegetable competition started at this time.

Men could enter up to three carrots, five potatoes and four cucumbers in the competition. Another category for miscellaneous veggies was added in the 1420s when some weirdly wonderful parsnips caused much mirth in a local hamlet. Prizes are awarded for the most anatomically correct vegetables.

The rules are very strict. Each vegetable must be entire of itself and can't have been carved, whittled, or artificially straightened in any way. Competitors can't glue vegetables together nor can they use specially shaped moulds to produce their obscene vegetables.

The most successful competitor was the 19th Century farmer Roger Myall, who won the carrot and cucumber competitions 12 years in a row. Rumours spread that Myall was in league with the devil, who, it was thought, pulled Myall's carrots downwards towards hell in exchange for Myall's soul when he died.

Harold Miget was the most unsuccessful competitor. He entered the miscellaneous vegetable competition 67 years in a row and failed to win a prize. He thought that his peas and Brussels sprouts were obscene in the eyes of God because of their round shape. The judges, who tended to be atheists, couldn't share this view and never awarded Miget a prize.

Cat Chasing in Barton-in-the-Beans

Barton-in-the-Beans is a village in the county of Leicestershire in the heart of England. In the Middle Ages it was believed that there were more cats in the village than in any other village or town in the country. This could only mean one thing in those times: witches. Lots of them.

There was no lake near the village. The local soil drained easily so even after heavy rain no large puddles formed. Thus deprived of his best known method of determining who was a witch, the regional Witchfinder-General Roger Boydell hit upon a novel method for searching out the local witches.

He determined that witches are very attached to their cats; at the equinoxes and the solstices he told his henchmen to round up all the village cats and place them into a large pen. At his signal, a man would allow three of the creatures to escape from the pen. These cats would be chased by the Witchfinder-General's fitter cronies around the village. If any woman chased after the man chasing her cat, especially on a broomstick, she was determined to be a witch and sent off to Leicester for burning on the High Cross.

This tradition lasted for 400 years, comfortably outlasting the role of Witchfinder-General by over 300 years. In the mid-20th Century, as people became aware of diets and exercise, it was noticed that the cats of Barton-in-the-Beans were the leanest, fittest, and most athletic cats in the whole county.

Gradually from all over the country owners of fat, unfit, and lazy cats brought their animals to the quarterly cat-chasing extravaganza. However, some of these owners refused to chase their cat through the village and both owner and cat were sent packing.

Other owners forgot their witch costumes and were disqualified. Distracted by the local mice population in the surrounding fields, some cats were lost forever. Sadly, some owners were as unfit as their animals and finished up at Leicester's High Cross hospital.

The Barton-in-the-Beans Cat Chasing is Leicestershire's largest group event and is held four times a year with around 500 cats participating over a long weekend. The sponsors of the event include Which? magazine and the Egyptian Embassy.

The Beltane Hound in the Isle of Man

Beltane or Beltaine is the anglicised spelling of the Old Irish Bel(l)taine or Beltine: the Gaelic name for either the month of May or the festival that takes place on the first day of May. Many fire festivals are held on this day to commemorate the days when people would traditionally burn their winter bedding and floor coverings. Other people celebrate Beltane because it's one of the two crossover days each year between equinox and solstice, the other being All Hallow's Eve.

The most interesting festival takes place on the Isle of Man when, in a strange twist to the crossover idea, men dress up as foxes and chase a foxhound across the island. The dog, known as the Beltane Hound, is usually the finest hound from Lord Laxey's kennels and the animal is given five minutes start ahead of the 50 or so foxes who chase it. Before the dog is allowed to leave, the foxes toast its health by consuming a small dram of whisky from the Glenkinnchie distillery. The dog is not allowed a drink.

The dog is released on the west coast of the island and the idea is that if the dog reaches the east coast then the men in the fox costumes each have to forfeit £100 to the ruling council of the Isle of Man, called the Tynwald. If one of the foxes manages to pin a pink rosette to the collar of the hound without being bitten then Lord Laxey has to pay forfeit to the Tynwald and also row a coracle around the Isle of Man in an anti-clockwise direction. The fox who pins the rosette on the foxhound receives the Stannary Cup.

The foxes are allowed to use public transport and bicycles but not private motorized vehicles to try and outmanouevre the hound. Likewise, nobody is allowed to conceal the foxhound or help it in any way. This relatively new ruling dates from 1873 when one of Lord Laxey's forefathers disguised that year's Beltane Hound as a pheasant, thus confusing the foxes. One of the more drunken foxes did admit that he came across the creature but mistook the dog's growling for a bad case of pheasant laryngitis.

There have been some unfortunate events. The 1911 Beltane Hound was never found and it was rumoured that it was aboard the Titanic heading for a new life. The 1954 Hound had no sense of direction and swam over to Northern Island. Three foxes had to be rescued by the local lifeboat as they tried to catch the creature. In 1968 one of the foxes had too much to drink and tried to pin his rosette to a police dog in Ramsay, the capital of the Isle of Man. The police dog's handler bit the fox, who had to be given a tetanus injection by the local vet as the town doctor was a teetotaller.

Marble Rolling in Carlisle

In Cumberland the ability to roll a marble an exact distance is highly prized. The climax of the marble rolling season is the Carlisle Round on the last weekend of August.

The roads around the centre of the city are closed for a week before the marble rolling so that they can be swept and the distances measured. There are 10 events held on different roads, ranging from the 10-yard nudge to the half-a-mile chuck. These distances are drawn between two lines on the road.

A yellow and green line is the starting line for all the events. No part of the competitor may cross this line otherwise the starter, known as The Reiver, will call "Foul Marble" and the competitor will lose their turn and be fined five grains of barley.

The aim of the event is to roll your marble so accurately that it stops on the line at the end of the course. This line is normally eight feet long and three inches wide or 'ye depth of a Scottish woman's bearde" as described in the original rules of 1517.

The idea is that the competitor with a marble closest to the line at the end of the event will win the prize of a haystack. Players can knock each other's marbles out of the way, but anyone who has a marble knocked off the line is entitled to another roll. This decision is made by the line judge or "Hadrian's spirit level" as he's known.

People come from all over the UK to play the Carlisle Round. Each person has their own method of making their marble perfectly round and free of imperfections. Some immerse their marbles in olive oil, others bake them in bread, and other rollers place them in an ice maker.

Joe Wharton has won more marble rolls than anyone else in the history of the Carlisle Round. His specialities were the 200-, 400- and 800-yard rolls, which he won every year from 1953 to 1972 due to an uncommon knack of slowing down his metabolism at the moment of delivery of the marble. Joe practiced so assiduously that he was run over twice by a delivery van when trying to practice in the early hours of a June morning. His competitors claimed he was gaining an unfair advantage by 'playing the course early' but there's nothing in the rules to stop this practice.

There have been some violent scenes in the past, when the Protestants accused the Catholics of celebrating too wildly whenever a green marble knocked an orange marble away from the line. Shouts of "that's for the Battle of the Boyne" were only the start of it.

The Pudsey Clog Festival

Clogs can be used in a surprising number of ways. The town of Pudsey has long been associated with the manufacture of clogs and it seems appropriate it is the host of the world famous Clog Festival. This festival has been in existence since 1613 and takes place on the fifth Saturday after the third full moon after Shrove Tuesday in odd-numbered years and on June 5th in even-numbered years. Festivals in even-numbered years are better attended for some unknown reason.

There are a huge variety of competitions. There is the clog-painting contest where prizes are awarded for using the most colours on one clog, the record for which is 274 by Mr Edward Goodge in 1871. Building a pyramid is the most onerous event, requiring a vast amount of clogs, so each team is limited to half-an-hour's building and at the end of the time the judges have to be able to discern a distinct pyramid. Towers and walls don't count. The highest pyramid ever was eight feet high, built by the Brighouse Working Women's Club in 1923 – they were said to have been inspired by the suffragette movement.

The most popular events are the athletics. 'Fetch thy Clog' is a favourite with whippet owners who train their dogs all year to retrieve a clog. The clogs are placed 100 yards from the start line. When the starting judge shouts 'dogs to the clogs' the whippets are released and race to their clogs; the first dog back gripping the right clog in its mouth wins the prize. However, the clogs are uniquely identifiable and if the winning dog brings back the wrong clog then it is disqualified. In this instance, the race is re-run. This might explain why the 1956 race took eight hours and was eventually won by a dachshund called

Molly, who was the only dog left from the original 223 competitors.

Other clog events include the 100-yard dash, the high jump, and the long jump. Competitors in the long jump must land in the sand still wearing their clogs otherwise a no-jump is declared. Then there's the throwing events including 'Lob the Clog' where the contestant stands in a shot putt circle and hops up and down on one foot three times before hurling the clog from his or her other foot. There's 'Welly the Clog' when people take a run up and then kick the clog furiously from their foot – on odd numbered years the event changes slightly in that the clog must knock over a cutout shaped like a Lancastrian archer, a throwback to the Battle of Towton when the Yorkist archers had to improvise after running out of arrows.

On the arts side, Pudsey's festival is also famous for the clog carving that takes place. The contests here include creating a matching pair of clogs for twins and a set of clogs for a greyhound so that it won't get foot rot during the winter months. These must be produced within the day using only traditional tools. Competitors are presented with blocks of wood at 9 a.m. and must have produced the clogs by 6 p.m.

Other artistic competitions include flower arranging using clogs, growing bonsai trees in clogs, and creating a wind chime for use in hurricane zones. There's also the painting competition entitled 'improve a famous painting by including a clog', which has proved controversial over the years, particularly when Albert Stuckle painted Munch's *The Scream* with a clog inserted in the mouth. Liberty has led the people wearing clogs, the *Mona Lisa* has worn a clog-shaped hat, and Monet's water lilies have become clogs floating on a pond. Mathilda Stevens was banned for life in 1936 for improving *The Naked Maja* in a rather painful manner.

Frog Racing in Bexley Heath

The racing of frogs is taken seriously in Kent. The *piece de resistance* is the Frog Derby in Bexley Heath on the third Saturday of June, which has been run since 1731.

The Frog Derby is run over an undulating course of 400 yards on the downs. At 8:55 a.m. 50 racing frogs are placed on the starting line by their trainers. Each frog is marked with a number so they can be identified. At 9 a.m. the starter shouts "frogs hop off" and the race begins.

The frogs must reach the finish line under their own power. The entire race course is cordoned off and no humans can enter this area during the race. This prevents trainers walking along in front of their frog with an enticing fly hanging on a string. This happened in 1782 when Josiah Smethhurst "coursed" his frog Bathsheba to the finish. Despite a protest from Toby Farquarson, the trainer of the Royal Racing Frog, Bonaparte, the result stood but the rules were changed to prevent it happening again. Trainers can place a carrot or other enticing tidbit at the finishing line for the frog to aim at but that's all that's allowed.

The course record is 4 minutes 36 seconds by Rupert the Racing Frog in 1862, a record he nearly broke in 1863. Rumours abounded that Rupert was 'gingered up' for both those races, an accusation with some substance given that he didn't stop at the finish line but carried on until he arrived at a pond and submerged in the water.

Besides the starting and finishing line judges there are a number of officials who take part in the event. Their names are Agincourt, Poitiers, Harfleur and Waterloo and their role is to keep the frogs in their place so that they don't leave the course.

Arrow Catching in the Staffordshire Moorlands and Matlock Bath

In days of old it was a huge honour to lead the nation's troops into battle.

This honour was decided by firing an arrow into the air from a longbow - whoever caught the arrow upon its return to earth would lead the line. Some knaves without armour did try and use their hands to catch the arrow but didn't appreciate its speed of flight and ended up with it embedded in their head, which meant they couldn't lead anything as they were dead. This is why knights were always heavily favoured to win the honour.

This tradition has led to two different annual events in separate parts of the English Midlands.

In the Derbyshire town of Matlock Bath, the arrow firing event takes place on Mad Wednesday, the first Wednesday after Easter Sunday. The general idea is that pubs from all around the Matlock area send teams to the event and if their team gets the arrow back to the pub before sundown then the pub wins a 56-gallon barrel of beer from the local brewery.

At 9 a.m. the longbowman stands in the middle of the town park and fires the arrow into the air. Each pub team is allowed to have one member in full armour who stands near the longbowman and watches the arrow and tries to catch it before anyone else when it returns to earth.

Once the arrow is under the control of one of the knights the judge shouts "held" and then everyone else involved in the contest is free to try to wrestle the arrow away from whoever has control of it. What normally happens is that a knight catches the arrow and runs off with it in the direction of his pub; he is then tackled by another knight and there's a huge scrum of metal bodies thrashing around on the ground. These are pulled away by other team members before the knight with the arrow is exposed and then pounced on.

If the arrow sticks into a knight instead of being caught the judge shouts "injured," the knight is replaced by another team member, and the arrow is fired into the air again.

In the Staffordshire Moorlands the event is run differently. On Walpurgis Day on Cannock Chase the longbowman fires many arrows into the air, one every 30 seconds for two hours, but all the individual contestants vie to catch the arrows on their own handheld targets. These are archery targets and the closer the arrow lands to the centre of the target the more points are awarded to the contestant. The winner is awarded a 30-gallon barrel of beer, which they must drink before the week is over.

Most contestants wear armour to reduce their chances of severe injury but some others, called whippets, wear no armour at all, which means they are far speedier around the playing area should the arrow be caught by a sudden gust of wind. They run a far greater risk of being injured but there are ambulances standing by to take the wounded to hospital.

The Pipe Cleaner Festival of Kirby Muxloe

Throughout the centuries the hobby of smoking a pipe has steadily declined. However, the usage for pipe cleaners has increased, largely because of the Kirby Muxloe Pipe Cleaner Festival.

A Pipe Cleaner is a strong metal wire covered in some material such as cotton, which can be easily bent into shapes or used to make sculptures.

At Kirby Muxloe this art form reaches its zenith on the 111th day of the year, which is almost always April 21st apart from in leap years. There are many different categories of pipe cleaner art. Competitors are allowed to colour their pipe cleaners before they begin their sculpture, but can't change those colours once the sculpture is complete.

The animal art is the most popular class. Walruses and elephants tend to be the most popular exhibits with their tusks as do giraffes with their long necks. The different sections are based on the number of pipe cleaners used. The 100-pipe cleaner section tends to produce smaller animals such as snails and cats, though Jeff Graham's "Very Bony Elephant" sculpture of 1983 was memorable for many reasons. The unlimited pipe cleaner class tends not to have too many entries, though Sara Smith's 1972 Blue Whale was chiefly memorable because it made the exhibition stand collapse under its weight. It was awarded the most life-like sculpture prize, though the money that went with the prize was withheld to help pay for the damage.

The festival started in 1813 - the first competition was mainly sculptures of the human form. Sculptures by men that claimed to be self-portraits and had massive wedding tackle were disqualified unless the judge, Lady Bellingham, found evidence to the contrary. In 1820 her husband divorced her when she told him how she uncovered this evidence and also that none of their six children were his.

Wilfrid Street holds the record for the person entering the competition for the most consecutive years, 62, and also for the least successful prize winner - 0. It's thought that his snail sculptures, although accurate, show little imagination, especially as he enters the same ones every single year.

Basil Cuthbertson was the most successful entrant ever; he won at least one prize in 14 consecutive years. He specialized in spiders and other insects and his *piece de resistance* was the 1912 scarab beetle, which used 4,000 pipe cleaners and is now on display in the Cairo Museum.

Hairy Legs Competition in Melton Mowbray

When people were painting the town red in Melton in the 15th Century some of the locals started to compare various parts of their bodies with those of other people. Eventually, the comparisons turned to the hairiness of the legs and it was noticed that a man called George Loveless had 'ye legs as hairy as that of a horse.' Loveless proclaimed himself as having the hairiest legs in Leicestershire and defied anyone to be hairier. He challenged all comers to a contest on the fifth Wednesday after Michaelmas on an annual basis – this was 1456 and the rest is history.

In the Hairy Legs competition there are a number of different sections to enter. There's a prize for the longest leg hair, another for the most amount of hair, and yet another for the most artistic shaping of leg hair. There are separate sections for men and women.

The longest leg hair ever measured was 3 feet 4 inches in length and belonged to Gwendoline Jones, a visitor to Melton, who entered the contest while waiting for a stagecoach to Nottingham in 1753. Gwendoline's legs were otherwise quite bare, but she did admit that this hair was a great source of pride to her and her family. She used to wash the hair in her monthly bath and treat it with sheep's oil to ensure that it didn't become brittle.

The men's record was 2 feet 9 inches grown by Alan Peacock in the 1870s. The hair was used to help keep his left sock up and he admitted to greasing it with pig's fat every night, which might explain why his wife left him for an arable farmer.

The hairy legs contest has changed with the advent of

cosmetic surgery. People have been disqualified in recent years when the judges have discovered that tufts of hair have been grafted on to people's legs, although this is more difficult to find than the amateurish attempts of Richard Davis in 1982, who, it was discovered, had glued cat hair to his knees. Davis was given a consolation prize of a tin of cat food and asked to pay his fine into the prize kitty.

For the genuine contestants, the judges comb the hair and discover the lushness and thickness of the fur. Contestants with fleas receive extra marks from the judges as this indicates genuine hair. The colour of the hair doesn't matter so contestants who dye their grey hairs don't impress the judges. The area the hair covers is also taken into account as is the location of the hair; furry knees, especially around the back, win high marks.

Competitors frequently use bizarre methods to encourage hair growth; Henry Travers, who won for 13 consecutive years from 1823-1835, swore by standing in a cow pat morning and night for 30 minutes – he is quoted as saying that "ye cowe patte contains growth – look how it makees the grasse become lushe." Travers never married during his life and lived alone in a house without running water.

Matilda Grinstead, who won the women's hairiest legs competition between 1901 and 1912, believed her success was down to bathing in baked beans every day – she ate the beans afterwards, which may explain why the judges inspected her legs through a telescope whenever possible.

Contestants' imaginations run riot in the leg hair sculpture competition, which started in the 1900s when sheep shearer Alex Shepley thought he would start shearing his own legs. For years Shepley's sheep had been the talk of the Midlands, with their immaculately shaped coats in three neatly trimmed lengths. Shepley had started out as a topiarist but was always disappointed that his hedges couldn't move. He turned to sheep shearing only after a brief flirtation with hedgehogs resulted in him being hospitalized with multiple punctures to the face.

Shepley thought of the leg hair sculpture contest when he was trimming his toe nails one day and thought that he could do the same with hair. Soon he had a hairy representation of Queen Victoria displayed on his left calf. A pork pie was shaved into his right thigh and soon Shepley was the toast of Melton. He displayed himself at the 1901 contest and was surprised to find that he was not alone in his shaving exploits. Respectable ladies had Gladstone and Disraeli shaved on their thighs; polite gentleman had coaxed representations of naked women from their lower legs – one lovelorn footman had the name of his employer represented on his hairy foot using a combination of glue and flour. The leg hair sculpture contest was born.

Pea-Shooting in Penistone

In the Middle Ages not everyone could afford a bow and arrow, so some poorer families became proficient with a pea shooter for self-defence. As Arnold de Sutcliffe said in 1562, "appen peas are cheaper than arrows and are easier to returne – some arrows gette stucke in things don't they ande breake, but them peas don't."

Accuracy with a pea-shooter is difficult, but the Penistone Pea-Shooting Prize Contest celebrates this accuracy over varying distances. The contest dates back to the Wars of the Roses when young Alec Ramsbottom protected his house from 50 Lancastrian soldiers with only a pea-shooter and 10 pods of peas. Ramsbottom's technique was to fill his mouth with peas and then fire them out rapidly, aiming at the mouths of the Lancastrians. He was so accurate that he succeeded in making each soldier swallow a pea; he then shouted, "them's plague peas them you Lanky bastards." The soldiers retreated to the nearest stream where they tried to regurgitate the peas, believing them to be detrimental to their health. This is one of the first examples of psychological warfare known to historians.

Nowadays contestants don't fire at Lancastrian tourists, but they do fire at two inch high lead soldiers lined up on a shelf three feet from the ground. The distances vary from 10 feet to 12 yards. Each pea-shooter can only be a maximum of three feet in length and can't be augmented by any devices that would increase the air pressure applied to the pea. "It must be all natural puff," says Robert Sidebottom, the current chairman of the contest, "using good natural Yorkshire air."

Each competitor is allocated 10 peas, dyed a colour that the contestant is completely unaware of beforehand, and has to knock down 10 soldiers in one minute. If the judges find any undyed peas then the contest is over for that shooter. This dyeing rule was introduced after the Albert Stubbs Controversy of 1843, when Stubbs knocked down his soldiers really quickly; however, when the judges picked up the peas for later use in the celebration lunch they found 33 peas. Under questioning, Stubbs admitted that he'd consumed five pods of peas before each round of the contest and was able to "returne them to my mouth withe easiness." Stubbs was banned for life and was prevented from growing peas on his allotment by the local council.

Kite Racing from Suffolk

Kites have been popular in Suffolk since their introduction into England.

In 1873, Oliver Helmes was flying his kite near Aldeburgh when the wind started to blow really hard – Oliver had difficulty holding on to his kite and thought that running with his kite would make it easier to control. This proved to be true. Oliver was seen by his friends and they tried running with their kites too. Soon a race was on, which was only brought to an end by a very aggressive bull called Bob.

Thus the Aldeburgh Kite Racing Festival was born. It's held in October and lasts for a week, during which racers have to be ready to race at all times. When the judges decide that the wind is strong enough for the longer races to be run to their conclusion, including the 10-mile Kite Marathon, then racers have 10 minutes to prepare.

The courses are over sand dunes, across dykes and through the Forest of Rendlesham. There are four races over 1 mile, 3 miles, 5 miles, and 10 miles. The winner is the person who crosses the finish line with his kite still intact and having not touched his kite during the race. This latter rule was introduced in 1897 after Jerry Payne hauled his kite out of the sky and carried it with him to the finish.

The competitors are limited to 100 feet of line, which is enough to clear the tops of the tallest trees in the forest. Most people believe that the best method for winning a race is to keep the kite on a short line through open country and then let the line out completely when approaching the forest. The runner's greatest skill is to pick a track through the trees that will keep the line clear of branches. Many a kite has been snared in the forest. Most of the fatalities in the race, apart from the drowning of Arnold Godber in 1932, have come from people falling out of trees when trying to rescue their kites.

John Vine has won the most races at the Kite Racing Festival, with 14 victories between 1922 and 1939. He was most adept at keeping his kite on a short line through the forest – defying conventional wisdom - thus reducing branch snaring to a minimum; for this he needed a strong wind and plenty of straight line speed in his running. In 1933, Vine won all four races and became the only person to complete the Grand Slam of Kite Racing. In 1967 Sally Smith won the first three races and was set to emulate Vine's achievement, but she ran into a tree on the 10-mile course and had to be taken to hospital still clutching her kite.

Contestants are not allowed to cover their line with anything sharp that could be used to cut the lines of other kites, as is done in kite fighting contests. This rule was introduced after the 1937 1-mile race when Mike Jones was the only person to finish the race; everyone else's kites had mysteriously been lost on their way because the lines had been cut. Jones claimed he'd seen an eagle attacking the other kites, but the judges were sceptical about this explanation, especially after Jones wouldn't let them see his line after the race.

Thimble Throwing from Accrington

In the mills of Lancashire, sewing fabric together with a thread from each new bale of cotton from North America was very important. In this way, the owners could determine how strong the cotton was and so they employed professional sewers to do it. The sewers were issued with a new thimble every six months to protect their fingers from the needles. If the sewer lost their thimble they had to pay for a new one, so there was a tendency to share the thimbles. In order to save time, thimbles were thrown from sewer to sewer. Some throws were more accurate than others, which led to thimble throwing contests on the annual works day out to Blackpool. This was first recorded in 1862 and the Thimble Throwing contest has taken place every year since then on July 5th in Accrington.

A 6-foot square is drawn on the ground and the contestants must try to land their thimbles in this area. Containers of varying sizes such as a bucket, a milk bottle, and an empty baked beans can are also placed in the area. The contestant wins extra points for landing their thimble in one of these receptacles – more points are awarded to contestants that land thimbles in the narrower receptacles, with the milk bottle being the highest points scorer. There are five rounds of thimble throwing and points are accumulated over all five rounds. In the first round contestants stand 10 feet away and in each subsequent round the distance is increased by a further three feet.

Betty Calthorp won the contest seven times between 1869 and 1891, largely due to her uncanny ability to throw her thimble into the milk bottle under pressure. She used an underarm delivery to ensure a high looping path for her thimble. This worked well in calm conditions but occasionally in high winds her thimbles landed outside the target area altogether. On the occasion of her seventh victory in 1890, she was awarded a milk bottle mounted on a piece of slate as a memento of her victories. The other multiple winner was Bill 'Beans Boy' Burns, who swore by aiming at the beans can at all times - his strategy led to five wins between 1922 and 1936.

In 1954, a second competition was introduced based purely on hurling the thimble the furthest distance from a fixed point using only human power. No slingshots are allowed. Each competitor uses a standard metal thimble without embellishment. This last rule had to be introduced in 1955 after the inaugural competition was marred by accusations of cheating. Some people filled their thimbles with wet sand while others attached wings and flew the thimble a long distance.

Some contestants use a shot putt technique to launch their thimble; others take a long run up *a la* javelin thrower and then hurl their thimble skywards. The longest distance ever recorded was 136 feet 4 inches by Dennis Taylor in 1972; it was a windy day and he determined that if he threw his thimble high enough the open end would catch a draught of wind and it would go further. He was proved correct and his record survives to this day.

The "She Loves Me, She Loves Me not" Contest - Exmoor

Fans of Lorna Doone believe that Exmoor is a romantic place and so many of them come with a dandelion and play the "she loves me, she loves me not" game – men blow the dandelion and say "she loves me" and then blow it again and say "she loves me not." The blowing continues until no seeds are left on the dandelion – then she either loves you or she doesn't. The same applies for the ladies.

In 1782, Amanda Barron and Elizabeth Bargeman both wanted a certain Amos Edwards to love them, so they stood side by side and played the dandelion game. Sadly, the dandelions showed that neither of them were loved by Amos, which was a relief to his wife and their four children. Thus, a contest was born.

Each contestant must bring a ready supply of dandelions that have their seeds showing. There are many rounds. The Shouting Judge shouts a number between 2 and 12 and then the Blowing Judge bids each contestant step forward in turn. This judge then shouts "dandelion be gone" and the contestant has to blow away all the seeds in the number of blows decreed by the Shouting Judge. If they achieve this, they are through to the next round. This process continues until there is only one person left who wins the Amos Love Cup.

There are separate contests for men and women. Only one person has won more than once: Eliza Bradley in 1803 and 1832.

A separate contest was spawned in 1898 when a distance element was introduced, with contestants having to blow away all the seeds from a dandelion in one puff while standing further and further away from the dandelion. This idea was born when a local called Ben Mergion was asked to blow out the candles on his birthday cake; Ben not only blew them out, he blew them off the cake, along with half the icing. Luckily, everyone whose face was covered in icing was feeling quite hungry that day. One of those present was the previous year's Shouting Judge, Barry Morgan, and he decided that the dandelion contest shouldn't just be about accuracy but about distance too.

Not surprisingly, Mergion won the first five distance contests with his record being 140 feet 8 inches in 1901. Later in life Mergion was employed by the RAF to start troublesome propeller-driven aircraft.

Fingernail Contest in the New Forest

It's rumoured that the main reason that the Normans invaded England in 1066 was for the truffle-hunting in the New Forest. The locals didn't need pigs to find truffles as they have always been possessed of fine long fingernails, which can quickly scrabble in the earth to find a truffle. Of course the truffles in the New Forest became extinct after overzealous hunting by the locals and the Norman invaders.

Although the truffles have gone the fine fingernails remain and are celebrated in the Fingernail contest held in Brockenhurst in September.

In honour of the truffle the main contest is a digging competition where people must use their bare hands to remove four feet of soil in as short a time as possible from an area a yard square. This contest takes place in hard ground where the initial incisions have to be made using the fingernails. Judges inspect the hands of the competitors before the contest to ensure that no-one has filed their nails to a point to gain advantage.

This contest was won six times in the 1930s by Bertie Smallman, who was held as a POW by the Germans during WWII but escaped by digging a 3-mile tunnel from his camp. After the war Smallman became an emergency gravedigger in the Hampshire area, who was called in either when epidemics overwhelmed the existing gravediggers or when he had to dig the grave of a fellow gravedigger.

The longest nail contest has been held since 1132. 10 prizes are given to individuals with the longest nail on each of the 10 fingers and thumbs. Individuals have their own ideas about how to grow a long fingernail: olive oil is used, as is baby oil and turpentine. A 16th Century vet, Jimmy Cowans, swore that placing his hand inside a cow's anus for 30 minutes a day hardened his nails wonderfully. Few people were prepared to disagree. Cowan did win five times between 1582 and 1598; however, more often than not at the time of the contest he had a very bad nosebleed due to his nervous habit of picking his nose and so was unable to take part in the contest.

There's also the pulling fingernail contest where people have to pull large weights along just using their fingernails. The objects used include ploughs, buses and Nell Gwynn, a local cow with a reputation for being bad-tempered. A rope is tied to the object and the contestant then digs their fingernails into the rope and pulls the objects along with their arms outstretched and their hands facing downwards, so that no muscle strength can be used.

In the dangling fingernail competition the contestant places their arm on a table with the fingernails hanging over the edge. The judge then dangles a weight from the nail for 20 seconds; if the nail breaks the contestant is eliminated otherwise they proceed to the next round where a heavier weight will be used. The record weight is 52 pounds, dangled from the left thumbnail of James 'Gurzel' Webster in 1812.

Seven-Legged Racing from Exeter

The festival of seven-legged racing takes place around the cathedral in Exeter on the third Thursday after the second full moon after Ash Wednesday.

The seven-legged race comprises teams of six people who race around the Cathedral exterior in an anti-clockwise direction. The prize is won by the first team to cross the finishing line having completed 66 laps. The race was started in 1541 by boys who had been unsuccessful in their attempts to join the cathedral choir and who wanted to put a curse on the building by invoking the spirit of the Antichrist with their 6 x 66 idea.

Initially, the teams were tied together with a rope that went around people's waists so that everyone had the use of both legs, but in 1652 the rules were changed by Cromwell, who wanted to make the race less fun and more puritanical by tying people's legs together. Thus the tradition was born which is maintained to this day.

At 8:30 a.m. the starting judge shouts to the teams, "bare ye legs." All shaving, lubricating, and massaging of the calves must cease and the Tying Men bind the runners' legs together using jute stripped from old sacks. The knots are very strong and won't come apart during the race. The teams line up at the start and wait for the starting signal. This is traditionally provided by a caw from the cathedral raven, Bertram, who sits on the shoulder of the Choirmaster, whose presence is a reminder to all participants of the original grievance of the boys in 1541. Some ravens are quieter than others so occasionally the race doesn't start until around 10 a.m. but typically the raven caws quite quickly and the teams are off.

Teams practice for months to find the necessary co-ordination between the team members, as this is an exhausting race if everyone isn't working together. There are some narrow sections between the gravestones in the cemetery, which require the teams to go along in single file but apart from this area the teams can run abreast. This is apart from the area outside the main entrance to the cathedral where the teams have to progress on their knees, observed closely by the kneeling judges, who penalize teams five minutes of time if all team members don't remain on their knees for long enough.

This kneeling section is another legacy of the Puritan era. It was introduced by Cromwell because he felt that the teams should be more deferential to the religious purpose of the cathedral. The kneeling judges in those times used whips to keep people on their knees for the requisite distance. Persistent offenders could be burnt at the stake as it was felt that people who couldn't stay on their knees for long enough must be having difficulty resisting the urge to fly and would therefore be witches in disguise.

The most successful team in the history of the race has been "Goldilocks and the Five Bears" who won 15 times between 1976 and 1995. The team would train for six months ahead of the race and practiced the kneeling part of the race assiduously, sometimes being mistaken for devout pilgrims by tourists. Other tourists would throw them money as they assumed the team were energetic beggars who needed financial help.

The Strathpfeffer Poetry Contest

The whole world knows about the Limerick, a five-line poem with a rhyming scheme of a,a,b,b,a. Fewer people have heard about the Strathpfeffer, which is an eleven line poem with the rhyming scheme a, b, c, d, a, b, e, e, c, d, e. The Strathpfeffer Poetry contest was founded in 1897 to make this poetry form known to a wider audience.

In this contest two schoolchildren are both asked to think of a number between one and 121. These two numbers are multiplied together and then a local Shakespeare historian, Dr Campbell Snoddy MacKenzie, finds that line number in MacBeth, who was born in the town. This line is then used as the first line of the Strathpfeffer. For example Dr Snoddy MacKenzie might select the line

But screw your courage to the sticking place,

The contestants would then have to compose their Strathpfeffer within 15 minutes of the line being read out:

For example, when the above line was read out by Dr Snoddy MacKenzie in 1968 the winner was a Mrs Doris McLeod of Dundee who wrote:

But screw your courage to the sticking place,
You know it needs an airing,
I will place mine up there too
And see how they get on
But this isn't a race
We will be sharing
And we will enjoy the sun
It will be fun
To see the sky so blue

Hoots mon
We'll even go for a run.

The only rules in the contest are that the poem must not contain any reference to "The Scottish Play" and must not contain any four-letter swear words. Poems that refer to "English bastards," Bannockburn or Stirling Bridge will get higher marks.

The only person to have won the contest more than once was Dr Hugh 'Sporran' MacDonald who won three times in a row from 1953 – 1955. Sporran was rewarded for weaving extravagant rhymes into his Strathpfeffers for words such as Sassenach, Highland Clearances, and Prestonpans. Sporran made his Strathpfeffers virulently anti-English, which went down well with the judges at least until 1956 when he rhymed 'might and main' with 'jugular vein' and was banned for life for parodying William McGonagall.

Sunrakers Festival from Dorchester

People from Wiltshire are known as Moonrakers. They used to keep their illicit alcohol in barrels and hide it underwater. They'd be seen by excise officers at night raking the barrels out of the water – when challenged they'd act stupid and say they were trying to rake the moon.

Not to be outdone, the people of Dorset thought they would like a nickname too and came up with the idea of calling themselves sunrakers. The problem was that no-one could come up with a plausible explanation for the expression. So was born the Dorchester Sunrakers festival.

Initially, the festival confined itself to people competing with each other to come up with either the most bizarre or the most plausible explanation for trying to rake the sun. As the years went by the festival expanded into a general excuses festival, where people came up with the most unbelievable excuses for various every day situations such as being absent from work, why their child can't come to school, or why they forgot about returning their library book.

The most popular contest is the Excuse of the Year award. This is given to the most ridiculous excuse for someone doing something they're not supposed to. In 1987, the winner was Miss Brenda Marlow from Doncaster who won for her famous retort to a traffic warden that her bike wasn't parked on the yellow lines: "my bike isn't parked illegally at all – my bike is parked between the yellow lines and no part of the tyre is touching the lines at all."

The Sunraker excuse contest is still going strong, although people who enter on a yearly basis can't repeat any of the previous excuses they have used otherwise they will be banned from the contest for life or "kept in the dark" as the rules say. This rule was introduced after Doris Randall from Dorchester kept giving the same answer year after year – the excuse was "because it's there" – and the judges couldn't stand it any longer and needed an excuse to ban Doris.

Some of the winning excuses as to why people would want to rake the sun include:

"So I could guarantee good weather on my summer holidays," "because I'd like to be getting a nice sun tan when I'm asleep," "so I don't feel so bad about suffering from insomnia," "every day will be Sunday and I won't have to go to work again," and "so my cat, who's half-blind, could find his way home at night."

Carrot and Stick Festival – Wimborne Minster

The carrot and stick approach has been defined as combining a promised reward with a threatened penalty although some people believe that the phrase should read "carrot on a stick," which is purely an incentive with no implied threat.

Both phrases have been incorporated into the Carrot and Stick festival at Wimborne Minster in Dorset, which has been an annual event since the days of Thomas More.

There are two main events at the festival as well as other attractions such as the "Look at my Big Stick" peepshow and the 'Interestingly Shaped Carrot" tent.

The first event is the Carrot and Stick throwing event. People taking part in this contest gather on the local green dressed in peasant clothing and carrying a stick with a nail in the end. This stick, which is checked by the measuring judge, must be no more than six feet in length. The idea is that carrots are catapulted into the air every five seconds via one of the siege engines used in this event. If a contestant manages to catch a carrot on his stick before it hits the ground then the contestant is through to the next round.

If a carrot falls to the ground and is then pierced by a competitor that person will be disqualified for cheating. People are not permitted to throw their sticks at a carrot in flight as this could be dangerous. Carrots are fired until there is only one person left without a carrot on the end of his stick. This person is eliminated. This process is repeated, often over several days, until either one person is left in the contest or the local supermarket runs out of carrots.

The person who won most often was the six feet seven inch tall Malcolm Cropper, who was victorious 23 times between 1732 and 1767. Cropper reportedly once said that, "my height was a big advantage to my success, but I also think that not drinking a vat of cider helped me line up the carrot with my stick." This gives an indication of the training methods of his fellow contestants.

The second contest is the Carrot and Stick event. Here contestants, called Jockeys, place a carrot on the end of their stick and then dangle it in front of a donkey that is pulling a small cart. This is supposed to entice the donkey forwards along the horseshoe-shaped course that the organizers lay out around Wimborne. It has to be the shape of a horseshoe as donkeys won't go past the place they first started from. Lots are drawn to see which driver gets each donkey. The start is in the old Le Mans style, where the drivers stand on one side of the High Street and at a signal from the Timer dash across the road, mount their carts, and start dangling their carrots. Some donkeys are fast starters and there have been occasional fatalities where slower drivers were knocked down by a ravenous donkey.

Frankie Turner won the event 12 times in his 40 years of trying, largely because he coated his carrot in honey which some donkeys adore. "Some years I win by a mile and at other times I don't even start because my donkey despises honey," said Frankie in 1998, a year before he was stung to death by irate bees in his apiary.

The most successful donkey was Billy the Swift, who won 14 times in his career between 1891 and 1909. Billy was born on a vegetable farm and loved his carrots. Upon his demise, Billy was stuffed (not with carrots) and placed in the Carrot and Stick Museum in Wimborne, which was built to commemorate the event.

Country and Western Air Guitar Contest – Morecambe, Lancashire

The singing of sad songs has been associated with Morecambe in Lancashire for hundreds of years. These dirges were usually sung when someone had been drowned in the dangerous waters of Morecambe Bay. These songs were sung so frequently that a competition was organized to see who could sing the saddest song of all. This contest reached its zenith with the 'Disaster' of 1812, when a man called Yeoman Parslow sang about the drowning of his wife and children in the Bay when they were trying to take a shortcut home after blackberry picking. His words were so heartfelt and his emotions so raw that two-thirds of the crowd were saddened to such an extent that they threw themselves into the sea too.

After this happened the contest was banned until 1963, when it was revived under the name the 'Country and Western Air Guitar Hoe-Down'. The contest is held in the third week of July, but only when the tide is out as a mark of respect to the events of 1812.

The format is quite simple. Every year 20 famous C&W artists are honoured in the contest. From Monday to Saturday two hours are set aside for three artists, whereas only two artists are featured on Sunday, again for two hours. The idea is that during these two hours people can sing one of the featured artist's songs while playing the air guitar, or sing one of their own songs in the style of that artist.

Judges wearing Stetsons and cowboy boots assess each performance – marks are awarded for the accuracy of the finger work on the air guitar, the accuracy of the impersonation and, where applicable, originality of the contestant's lyrics. Few people will forget the poignancy of the following song written by Benny "Wail On" Lee in the style of Waylon Jennings from the Wednesday contest in 1987.

"My dogggeeeeee got run over by the undertaker,
Taking my wife's body to the morgue,
Ah would have waved her goodbyeeeeeee,
But my arms got pulled off,
In a farm accident,
Last weeeeeeeeeeeekkkkkkkk,
My grand daddy's heart broke in two
When the crops failed,
For the fifth straight year,
But despite all these disasters
I still go to church,
Even though I can't pray now
Because my arms got pulled off
In a farm accident,
Last weeeeeeeeeeeekkkkkkkk,"

After Benny sang the song a large number of people were in floods of tears and heading towards the pier, but were stopped by the police who sprayed them with nitrous oxide.

Multiple winners at the contest include Roger Donnelly who impersonates Fatboy Slim Whitman, Wendy Berenson who sings the songs of Willy Nelson with a broad Yorkshire accent and above all Timmy Waites, whose variations of Tammy Wynette's song D.I.V.O.R.C.E have to be heard to be believed. In the 1980s his winning efforts included the cunning protest songs

T.H.A.T.C.H.E.R.O.U.T,
S.C.A.R.G.I.L.L.F.O.R.E.V.E.R and the 17-minute long *S.U.P.P.O.R.T.T.H.E.M.I.N.E.R.S.A.G.A.I.N.S.T.T.H.E.F.A.S.C.I.S.T.D.I.C.T.A.T.O.R.T.H.A.T.C.H.E.R.*

Spoon Balancing from Todmorden

In times past life was hard for the poorer people in British society. Working in the fields was a tough life, especially when the weather was bad. Most families lived from hand to mouth and at mealtimes there were no kitchen implements to help consume the food.

With this background you can imagine the surprise that Reg Wormold had in April 1782 when he came across a spoon at a fork in the road. Reg didn't know it was used for eating food. He tried balancing it on his finger and he also placed the curved end on his nose and walked along. Each day he became more proficient at these games until he thought he was the finest spoon balancer in the business.

On September 1st 1782 he nailed a piece of wood to the pub door, on which was written in charcoal the words "ye conttestte bee announced – nextte Saterrday."

On that Saturday Reginald stood on the town green brandishing his spoon and challenging anyone to balance the implement on their nose for longer than he could. Thus was born the Todmorden spoon balancing competition.

Today, the contest attracts people from all over the world where spoons are used. There are two ways that people's spoon balancing skills are challenged. The first is when competitors balance a spoon on the end of their finger (any finger will do – Reg Wormold only had five fingers and one thumb due to farm injuries). While balancing the spoon on their finger the contestant has to stand on one leg and then after five seconds transfer their weight to the other leg. The person who does this for the longest time will win the prize of a set of steak knives.

The other contests relate to balancing the spoon on the nose. There are a number of races over distances from 100 yards to one mile. There's also a sack race of 400 yards and a three-legged race of 250 yards. The rules are simple: if the spoon falls off the nose the contestant must immediately stop, pick up the spoon, and retreat five paces before placing the spoon back on their nose and re-commencing the race. People have cheated by gluing the spoon to their nose using sticky substances such as mucus, cement, and plaster. The rules state that at the end of the race the Unspooning Judge has to remove all spoons personally to check to see whether any illegal substances have been used.

Emily Jackson is the champion spoon balancer, having won the one mile race every year from 1871 to 1881. She attributed her success to "good old-fashioned Yorkshire grit and plenty of spittle on the spoon, but not so much that any of it goes to waste." She had to retire in 1882 because of a neck injury resulting from her preferred running method, which was to run with her head almost parallel to the ground. Jackson still holds the one mile race record of 5 minutes and 34 seconds.

The sack race is the most difficult race of all because of the jarring when both feet hit the ground at once. In 1862 Seth Sidebottom tripped up during the race and the spoon somehow finished inside his nose when he hit the ground, necessitating a trip to the local hospital. In 1900 , two competitors, one from Ramsbottom and the other from Barnsley, collided during the race resulting in much bad feeling and shouts of, "remember Towton."

The Lady of the Lake Contest – Crummock Water

It's hard to say how this contest began or when – some people say it's proof that King Arthur was from the Scottish Borders region; others believe that the contest only dates from the 1600s when women were thrown into lakes to determine whether they were witches.

The Lady of the Lake contest takes place on the fourth Sunday in June at Crummock Water in the Lake District. The contest is divided into 10 separate throwing events – the shortest of 10 yards, the longest of 100 yards. Nowadays, the 10 Ladies of the Lake are determined by numerous endurance contests at various swimming clubs in the Lake District. In olden times, when there were no such things as diving suits, everyone from the local village would take turns being the Lady, so as to stop anyone from getting hypothermia. When the water was really cold the Lady of the Lake would sit on a log.

At 8 a.m. the Lady of the Lake for the 10-yard throw waddles into the water and swims to her appointed spot for the first round of the contest. When she's in the correct place, the throwing judge, or Sir Gawain as he's known, shouts "King Arthur be here". The Lady then extends her sword to its full length. At this point the contestants are allowed to start throwing their quoits in an attempt to land them on the sword. Each person has 10 quoits and has 20 minutes to throw them all.

The person who lands the most quoits over the sword wins the prize of a carving knife for the Christmas turkey. If there is a tie then contestants have a sudden death throw-off, taking alternate shots at the upright sword until one person lands a successful throw. Once a winner is determined, the 10-yard Lady is replaced by the 20-yard Lady and the contest is resumed using exactly the same rules.

The most successful thrower of all time was the 18th Century blacksmith Jebbediah Jennings, who won at least two contests per year between 1714 and 1756. He attributed his success to a steady hand and lots of practice. He described his technique thus, "I sees no point in chucking ye quoit on a flat track as it bain't going to hit the mark; my idea is to swing my arm in line wit'swordde, throw it high and make sure it's going end over end towards ye pointed end; the flat of't hand should finish high, like I was waving to the sun or a passing clouded."

In 1861, there was a huge altercation because one of the contestants, Hugh Burley, had recently been jilted by the 30-yard Lady of the Lake and so he threw his quoits at her, hitting her on the head. She responded by throwing the quoits back, hitting Sir Gawain and two other contestants. She then swam to the shore and chased Burley, stabbing him in the buttocks four times before being restrained.

To stop this happening again, four knights, Sir Bedivere, Sir Lancelot, Sir Bors and Sir Galahad patrol the throwing area and are allowed to smite any wrongdoer who is attempting to hurt the Lady of the Lake.

Australia Day – Northampton

The Northampton sheep thief, George Bellamy, was the first person to ever return from Australia after escaping from the penal colony in 1788. Despite his claims of having swum back, it's thought that he stowed away on a Dutch East India slave ship from Indonesia to the Cape Province, from where he made his way back to England.

He brought back tales of strange animals such as the kangaroo and the wallaby that jumped around on their back legs. His impressions of these animals caused much mirth and led to much mimickry, as did his description of the boomerang and the didgeridoo.

On the first anniversary of his return it was decided to hold a contest in his honour. There was the category of best impression of a kangaroo or a wallaby, which was judged by Bellamy himself. This category resulted in a mass brawl when one of the entrants, Elias Wollingford, rather enthusiastically jumped into a cowpat, spraying the other contestants, who took objection to his tactics.

In the late 1960s this category was widened due to the popularity of the hit TV show Skippy the Bush Kangaroo. People had to do their best impression of Skippy conveying information to the authorities, which largely comprises people opening and closing their lips in rapid succession while making kissing noises. A storytelling element, called "What's that Skip?" was also added where the contestant had to come up with the most ridiculous and long-winded sentence that could be conveyed by a kangaroo – a good example would be the winning 1971 entry as follows: "What's that Skip? The bad guys, one six feet high, the other five foot 10, are heading this way in a blue and white checked pickup truck whose leftside rear tyre is low on pressure and which will run out of gas in 12 miles, if they don't fill up at the gas station in Woollamaloo before midnight."

Another element of Australia Day is throwing the boomerang. Originally people just threw any piece of wood into the air, not realizing that the wood has to come back to them. George Robinson was disqualified in 1821 for using his retriever dog to return the wood – this was deemed to be an infringement of the spirit of the contest.

In 1862, Jeffrey Smeruy achieved the first return flight of a boomerang, although due to short-sightedness his attempt to catch the returning object left him with a broken nose and concussion. Smeruy's design was soon copied by everyone else, which led to the contest of 1863 being fondly remembered as the Headache Year. All the entrants threw their boomerangs at the same time and the first one back won the prize, as long as it was caught by the owner. At a signal from the Hurling Judge the 185 entrants threw their Smeruy-designed wooden objects into the air. The boomerang has to be thrown at the correct angle and not with great force otherwise its arc will be too wide. Of the 185 throwers, it's estimated that 87 had the correct technique and their boomerangs arrived back en masse, causing people to run into each other; some people were hit by a boomerang and some caught the wrong one, leading to both disqualification for interference and a pummeling from the owner, whose chance for victory had also gone.

The winner was announced as James Sidney, although he was unconscious at the time and had his boomerang wedged in his mouth. By sheer luck Sidney had unintentionally intercepted his own boomerang with his teeth – the good news was that he won the prize of a year's supply of chickens, the bad news was that he would have to eat soup for the rest of his life – chicken soup for the sole winner of the contest.

In subsequent years, the boomerangs were thrown individually and the one with the longest flight time won the prize of a soup bowl with matching soup spoon, known as the Sidney Soup Set or SSS for short.

The last element of Australia Day is the didgeridoo contest, which has two separate parts. The first is where entrants have to play either a classical piece of music such as Swan Lake or a medley of pop hits by groups such as The Beatles, Abba, or Elvis Presley. 12 judges then mark their efforts for accuracy and artistic merit. The three highest scorers have to perform the same piece of music in the final and the winner is the person who garners the highest marks from the judges. Josiah Applegate's rendition of Beethoven's Moonlight Sonata in 1956 is still remembered for its lilting qualities and had many people in tears.

The other didgeridoo event is the 'Make a Noise' competition. Contestants make a didgeridoo out of unlikely components such as flower pots, downpipes, or cardboard boxes and then attempt to play them like a didgeridoo. Nobody can use the same instrument twice in the contest, which makes the feat of Mark Rochester quite remarkable. He won this contest for 23 years in a row from 1959 to 1981 using an amazing variety of designs. Just before the 1982 contest he was taken to hospital with severe concussion after dislodging a slate roof tile from his neighbour's house after trying to steal his downspout for use in the contest. The suspicions of the police were aroused and they found an Aladdin's Cave of stolen property in Rochester's garage. Whisky bottles, tubes, drains, pipes, flower pots, gutters, safety cones, chimney pots and pottery mugs were found in abundance. Now the rules state that everyone entering this contest must produce a receipt detailing the components of their didgeridoo.

Bicycle Mending in Yeovil

Ever since inner tubes were placed inside bicycle tyres there's been the problem of how to mend them in the quickest possible manner. The most common solution is to remove the inner tube and place it in a bowl of water and squeeze the tube lightly so air bubbles come to the surface from the offending puncture.

The culmination of the art of puncture repair is found at the Bicycle Mending festival in Yeovil, held in the third week of June every year.

People from all over the country come to Yeovil to test their skills. Each competitor is handed a bicycle, both of whose tyres have two punctures and so is completely unrideable. These punctures have to be fixed in the quickest possible time and the contestant has to ride their bike around a 10-mile course to test how well they have fixed the inner tubes. This latter ride prevents unscrupulous competitors from filling their inner tubes with glue or coating them with clumping cat litter, as happened in the early days of the contest. The winner is the person who crosses the line first in the cycle race.

The competition started in 1906 and there are separate events for men and women, which are then divided into separate contests based on age: these contests are for under 25s, 26 – 40, 41 – 55, and 56 and over.

The champion fixer has been Harry Creighton – born in 1914 - who won first prize in his age class every year between 1934 and 1976, with the exception of 1956 when he was in hospital with a punctured lung after he'd fallen from his bike practicing for the contest. Harry's big trick was to submerge the inner tube in a large bowl, find the punctures, and then quickly cover the holes with masking tape, which saved time compared to using glue and patches. Harry was also very wiry and a strong cyclist.

Monica Sullivan is the most successful female cyclist, having won 12 age group races during her career. She is most famous for a spectacular crash in the 1972 race when her patches failed to hold on a steep downhill section and she cartwheeled into a stream, causing disruption to an angling competition. She was hooked by a fisherman as she floated past and he claimed her as a catch, but the judges disqualified his claim because he hadn't landed her on the bank using a fishing net.

The Ludlow Catching Acorns and Conkers Festival

Autumn is the time when items fall from trees with great regularity. Acorns and conkers can be caught in large numbers. In Ludlow in the first week of October there's a festival that tests contestants' catching stamina to the full.

This is the Ludlow Catching Acorns and Conkers Festival, a contest that takes place between the hours of 6 a.m. and 7 p.m. on seven consecutive days. The trees used in the festival are either English oak trees or horse chestnut trees and a different tree is used each day.

The number of contestants is limited to 30 people each year, so that they can all fit comfortably under one tree. These people comprise the top 20 catchers from the previous year's contest plus 10 others who have come through the regional pre-qualifying rounds. Competitors can only wear a smock without pockets during the event and are always strip-searched before competition begins to ensure they aren't concealing any acorns or conkers about their person. Acorns and conkers are referred to as tree fruit at the festival.

The idea behind the contest is that the competitors stand under the tree and try to collect the tree fruit that fall before they hit the ground. Anyone who picks up an acorn or conker after it's hit the ground will be disqualified by one of the Seeing Judges, who stand under the tree. These judges also keep a tally of those contestants who have caught a tree fruit and then they remove the fruit from the playing area so that it can't be reused by an unscrupulous contestant.

This was the result of the Barry Jackson affair of 1846 –

Jackson used to catch the fruit, store them in a bowl, and then throw them up in the air again when no-one was looking. He'd catch the fruit and so score another point. He was only found out on day five after claiming to have caught an acorn under a horse chestnut tree. He was banned for life with immediate effect and went back to his previous job as the official Village Idiot in nearby Church Stretton.

The most successful contestant was Roger Silas who won the festival in 1782, 1788 and 1801 – the only person to have won three times. He was like lightning and not averse to throwing himself full length to catch the tree fruit just before they hit the ground. His winning haul of 511 acorns and 312 conkers in 1788 is still a record. He trained for the event by standing under trees in the local park for three days straight and staring upwards at all times. Alas, this behaviour stayed with him for the rest of his life and he was run over by a train near Birmingham in 1838.

The biggest scandal, even surpassing the Jackson affair, was the Biggs Jackdaw Scandal of 1891. Thomas Biggs thought that he could win by training his pet jackdaw, Reuben, to jump around in the tree above his head and so either loosen the tree fruit or throw them to Biggs when he was on his own under the tree. This worked for the first three days until a judge saw the jackdaw throw a conker to Biggs as he leaned against the trunk of the tree. Both Biggs and Reuben were forbidden to take part in the festival for the rest of recorded time. Biggs never recovered from the ignominy of his ban and died in solitude in Gloucester in 1912. However, Reuben made a living by starring in his own dart throwing show at local fairs.

The Acorn and Conker Catching Contest has an interesting rule whereby if no acorn or conker has fallen for an hour then the Chief Counting Judge shouts "release the squirrels." The Squirrel Containment Officer then releases five squirrels into the tree. The idea is that the activity of the squirrels ensures that some tree fruit are disturbed and fall towards the ground. These squirrels are kept in a cage during the contest and released back into the wild once it's over.

There have been some accidents, largely when people charge into each other when trying to catch the same tree fruit. Others have suffered eye injuries when misjudging the velocity of a falling conker, especially from the Cripple Horse chestnut which is over 200 feet high. As recently as 2007, a competitor had to be rushed to hospital after swallowing a conker that had deflected from another contestant's head. This is why the Health and Safety Executive encourages participants to wear facial masks at all times as well as knee and elbow pads.

Roger Silas best summed up the spirit of the festival when he said "Ye conteste had made me loiffe compleeet and Oive started many friendships under them trres, which have lasted a loifetime."

The St Andrews Seed Sessions

Most people think nothing of mundane activities such as spitting out a seed, flicking a discarded pip from a trouser leg, or squeezing a cherry stone between your fingers until it scoots into the distance. However in St Andrews in Fife these activities are celebrated in style at the annual Seed Sessions in the third week of August.

The term 'seed' is a generic term that covers pips, stones and hulls from various fruits. Because of the different sizes of the seeds, each of the contests is split into categories for apple seeds, orange pips, cherry stones, olive pitts and watermelon seeds.

The methods used to propel the various seeds are spitting, squeezing between two fingers and flicking from a flat surface with a finger. There are accuracy tests as well as distance contests.

The festival started during the annual apple picking in 1847 when young men in the orchard were spitting out the pips from their Red Victoria, Cambusnethan Pippin and Lord Grosvener apples. One youth, Iain Logie, maintained he could spit a pip further than anyone else, although this was difficult to prove as all the pips looked the same. Jamie Nesbit said he could decapitate a wasp at 10 paces using a pip that he spat from his mouth.

As no headless wasp bodies could be found, it was decided to organize a contest and have judges to act as independent witnesses. When the Wasp Protection League objected to the possible massacre of these insects in St Andrews it was decided that people should instead aim at matchsticks stuck in wax.

For the distance contests jute sacks from nearby Dundee were used as the playing area covered an area 100 yards square. The distances were marked at every foot and the distance was counted as where the pip finished up rather than where it initially landed, thus allowing the exponents of the 'bouncing bomb' technique to compete on equal terms against the high trajectory spitters, flickers and squeezers.

Once orange pips were added to the contest in 1920 then the landing area had to be trebled in area due to their extra weight and more rounded shape. Soon cherries, olives and watermelons were added to the list of seeds. In subsequent years, larger stones such as those found in apricots, nectarines and avocadoes were tried as 'guest' seeds but have never been accepted into open competition. This is due to the large amounts of phlegm accompanying the seeds when they were spat out of a contestant's mouth. There was also a near tragedy in 1956 when a contestant, Archie McFadden, swallowed an avocado stone he was meant to be spitting and had to be rushed to hospital because of breathing impairment.

Competitions for each fruit's seeds are contested on separate days allowing generalists and specialists to compete on equal terms. Seeds travel furthest in the squeezing events. The overall distance record is the 474 feet seven inches that an orange pip travelled in 1928 after it had been squeezed between the middle finger and thumb of Dougal MacDonald from Lossiemouth. MacDonald was accused of cheating by fellow competitors as the pip had been aerodynamically carved beforehand, so competitors are no longer allowed to bring their own seeds with them. Instead they are allocated a pip or seed from a variety of their choice and must use it otherwise they are disqualified for time-wasting.

The spitting contests are normally the least popular with spectators because of the potential inaccuracy of amateur spitters. Judges wear gloves and surgical masks to reduce the chances of contamination; all seeds are removed using either tweezers or calipers and are then burnt, unless a record has been set in which case they are sent to the spitting museum and planted for prosperity. The record for spitting a seed is 368 feet two inches by Mrs Elsie Anderson of Tobermory, whose record has stood since 1921. She spat a pip from a Red Victoria apple using her tongue to apply topspin in a technique she referred to as 'tossing the caber.' Apples from this tree fetch a high price from contestants anxious to win a prize; since 1921 pips from apples grown on this tree have been used by eight winners of the Apple Pip spitting contest and are thus justly regarded as the thoroughbreds of the apple pip world.

The accuracy contests take place over distances ranging from five to 50 yards. Five matches are stuck into wax and contestants have to knock down as many as possible using a maximum of 10 seeds in the quickest time possible. Extra points are awarded if the match is ignited by the seed. Again contestants spit, flick and squeeze their seeds at the targets.

The legendary Elsie Anderson holds the record for the apple pip spitting accuracy contest, scoring 806 points in 1922 when she ignited all five matches in five seconds from a distance of 20 yards using her 'Highland Fling' technique. This involves rolling her tongue around the pip and blowing hard to impart sidespin before spitting the pip at the target.

Elsie Anderson's mother knew her daughter would excel at these events as she had shown promise from an early age: "why, when Elsie was seven years old, we baked her a cake and put the candles on and lit them. When she tried to blow them out she blew them clear off the cake, setting fire to the cat and the curtains. The icing finished all over the wall and the wee decorations smashed the plates on the dresser."

Not all contestants have been as successful as Elsie Anderson. In 1968 Walter Nesbit from Crianlarich recorded the shortest distance ever for a seed squeeze – six inches. His explanation was as follows: "somehow the seed moved between my thumb and forefinger so that it came out upwards rather than forwards – the seed rebounded off the end of my nose and barely made it over the starting line – I was so embarrassed." What Mr Nesbit failed to mention was that all his previous attempts had gone up his nostrils and hadn't registered any distance at all.

The champion flicker of all time is Jock Macduff from Strathpfeffer, who won every apple, orange and watermelon flicking contest between 1937 and 1967. He used to soak his fingernails in vinegar when he was out of competition so that they would be hard as leather during the flicking contests. He used the 'bouncing bomb' technique for orange pips and the high trajectory flick for apple and watermelon seeds. All seeds were balanced on the right knee of his moleskin trews before the force was applied by his fingernail. The trews were his lucky charm and he never washed them from year to year, so that by 1968 they were deemed to be a health hazard by the judges and he was banned from competing.

Tossing the Cricket Stump in Cockermouth

The annual Tossing the Cricket Stump contest in Cockermouth dates back to 1856 when cricket first came to the town. Three local vicars had visited the Scottish Border Games in Galashiels the previous year and seen the tossing of the caber contest there.

Inspired by the athleticism of the Scots – and some beer according to the gossip-mongers – two of the vicars attempted to lift the caber. One, Hugh Fotheringham, suffered a ricked back, which left him unable to preach for six months. The second vicar, Abel Soames, lifted the caber and tossed it into the air. Unfortunately his caber didn't land properly and rebounded backwards, hitting him on the head and rendering him unconscious. His final words were reputedly "I thought this only happened to beavers." He was laid to rest by the third vicar, the strict Methodist Ebenezer Wesley, who was tee-total.

In Soames' honour it was decided to hold a commemorative contest every year that would provide a skilful and yet safe test for local people. It was deemed appropriate that this test should involve throwing something. Tossing the caber was ruled out and the only pieces of straight wood in the town, other than trees, were the cricket stumps, so it was decided to hold a stump throwing contest.

As in caber tossing the objective is not how far you throw the stump but how straight it lands. The contestants hold the stump by the sharp end with both hands and throw it up into the air with enough momentum so that the blunt end hits the ground and then topples over so that the sharp end is pointing away from the thrower.

The judges measure the straightness against magnetic north on the compass and award points for accuracy and direction. Placing magnets in the cricket stump doesn't help point the stump at magnetic north. This was proved in 1867 when Harold Streete, the town idiot, buried magnets in his stump and then tossed it skywards. The additional weight caused the stump not to rotate properly and it became buried in a molehill. Ebenezer Wesley's wife, Henrietta, took one look at the sight, reportedly said "wow," blew out her cheeks, and then fainted. Wesley accused Streete of "ye devil's work" and ordered him to be banished from the town for "ye rest of recorded time." Since 1867 the person coming last in the contest has received "Streete's Award."

Some people have tried throwing the stump with one arm but straightness can't be guaranteed with this technique, especially if the stump hits a seagull as happened in 1985. It took four people to get the angry bird to the vet where the stump was removed after a lot of blood had been spilled. Nowadays, the gulls watch the contest from the roof of the cricket pavilion.

Armour Making from Ashby-de-la-Zouch

The tradition of making armour for battle goes back thousands of years. Strapping leather together to make a strong material resistant to bronze sword blows was probably the first type of armour ever created. Leather was replaced by chain mail and then this was superseded by full suits of armour made from steel and iron, so heavy that their wearers couldn't regain their feet if they fell off their horse.

All these forms of armour are celebrated at the Armour Making Contest at Ashby-de-la-Zouch, which is held on the Sunday nearest to August 22nd, the day that the nearby Battle of Bosworth took place in 1485.

There are many different categories to enter. The most popular is the chain mail contest where rings of metal are joined together to form a strong protective barrier against sword thrusts and arrows. There is a children's version of the contest where kids link paper clips together in playful imitation of the real thing. A knitting contest also takes place with the aim of producing a half-length chain mail coat made from wool within three hours.

The contest started in 1685 to mark the 200th anniversary of the Battle of Bosworth and the succession of the Roman Catholic King James II. In the first year there were only two contests – the leather armour one and the chain mail for men. Contestants had "ye lengthe of burnningge of a six inch candle" to complete their armour. The armour then had to be tested; the original idea was for the local Protestant vicar to put on all the armour in turn and then be attacked by the largely catholic judges with swords until the vicar screamed for mercy. This idea was vetoed by the town's mayor who decided that it was in the best interests of religious tolerance for the armour to be tested on a tree stump.

The first winners were Miles Cronden in the leather contest and Paul Merrill in the chain mail. Cronden hardened his leather in urine and according to the judges "ye stenche was exceeding stronge and diluted thy desire to be neare." Merrill was an exceptional blacksmith whose designs for chain mail were tightly packed and so strong that some swords were blunted on them. Two hundred years later one of Merrill's direct descendants, Josiah, was the first winner of the chain mail knitting contest.

A tree stump is still used to test every contestant's leather and chain mail armour to this day despite suggestions from the organizers of the barbecue in the 1970s that perhaps their meat could be fresher and more tender if pigs and cows were used for testing.

Over the years more contests were added for men and women including the *piece de resistance,* the full body armour contest, which is awarded for work done during the previous year. Points are awarded for historical accuracy, but the ultimate test is for the contestants to walk across the Bull's Field belonging to Farmer Grinlow and see how well their armour stands up to the attack of the Aberdeen Angus purebreds. The judges note how quickly the bulls give up their attacks, how many dents the armour has sustained, and whether the contestant needs medical help afterwards.

David Graham is the best builder of full body armour in the country and has won on six occasions since 1996. He uses stainless steel coated with tungsten and zinc, all of which is highly polished – it has been suggested that this is deliberate so that the bulls will be blinded by the sun glinting off the metal, but Graham still won after the bulls were fitted with sunglasses.

There was almost a tragedy in 1948 when Sir Lawrence

Hislop entered the contest. His armour was the Tin Man costume worn in the 1930s film The Wizard of Oz, which Hislop had recently bought at auction. The costume was flimsy at best and Sir Lawrence was knocked unconscious as soon as he entered Bull's Field. Luckily, his wife and daughters dragged him clear whilst the bulls were being distracted by a Judy Garland impersonator.

The knitting contest has been won most often by local shepherd Wilf Worrall, who won 12 times between 1872 and 1910. He used wool from his own sheep to create the imitation chain mail. He practiced his technique out in the fields and honed his skills so well that he could produce a full set of imitation chain mail in just 90 minutes. His concentration on the knitting was legendary, but this did mean his sheep were left unsupervised and he lost 30% of them to rustlers on average throughout the year.

Christmas Tree Topiary from Northallerton

At the end of the Christmas holidays in the dark days of winter everyone needs to let off a little steam. This may explain why the Christmas Tree Topiary contest in Northallerton is so popular with people eager to reshape their Christmas trees after spending many tedious and argumentative hours with their families.

On January 5th, people come to the main street of the town with their trees and then between 8 a.m. and 9 a.m. they can register for the topiary contest in one of three categories of shaping device: nail clippers (for trees under three feet high), scissors and secateurs (for trees under 10 feet high), and chainsaws (10 feet and over).

The contest started in 1862. The chainsaw category, added in 1978, replaced the kitchen knife category, which was dropped from the contest at the advice of the police after the 1977 contest ended in bitter recriminations and much bloodletting. Obviously families had been hard to deal with that Christmas.

At 10 a.m. sharp competitors are allocated a place on the main street and asked to place their trees in this area. At 10:15 the Cutting Contest Chief shouts "prepare thy implements for carving" and then one minute later he continues, "start to cut." The contestants then have four hours to shape their trees into something recognizable and aesthetically pleasing.

There are some very strict rules: competitors can't interfere with the carving of anyone else's tree even if they think that something rude is being shaped, though they can draw the Taste Judge's attention in such an eventuality.

Anyone producing an offensive display can be disqualified *sine die* if the object is deemed to be unsuitable for public viewing. An example of this happened in 1971 when Sidney Hines' attempt to carve a penis was thwarted by the Taste Judge despite Sidney's claims that it was a Saturn V rocket with unusually shaped fuel tanks.

No-one is allowed to bring any sprays into the contest area. This rule is in place to stop defoliants spoiling the contest. This was after an anti-Vietnam War protest in 1967 when several people tried to infiltrate the contest area with bottles containing Agent Orange. The protest might have been successful if they hadn't been shouting "stop bombing Laos" and wearing masks whilst carrying their Christmas trees.

Two people have dominated the contest over the years. Angela Spratt won the nail clipper contest 17 times between 1932 and 1961, carving beautiful birds and squirrels from her trees with great skill. She used Christmas decorations to represent the animals' eyes and plumage or fur to great effect. Her greatest achievement was a lyre bird, which won in 1952. This carving scored 98 out of 100 in each of the three judging classes: technical achievement, tastefulness, and artistic merit.

Dan Smethurst won the scissors contest 16 times in the period 1891 to 1919; he was the local barber and had a tendency to practice on his customers during the year by way of preparing for the event. His favourite subjects were dogs and his carvings of canines were both life size and accurate. In the 1910s he concentrated on creating poodles, which won him many contests but lost him many customers as people didn't appreciate having a haircut with small rounded balls lining their head.

There has been some controversy in the contest, largely because of the Minimalist School of Topiary and their belief in the Green Pyramid system. They maintain that a Christmas tree is a work of art in itself and doesn't need to be changed much by the shaper for it to be beautiful – they decree that a tree shaped like a Green Pyramid is the perfection of nature and should be judged as such at the contest.

Mike Johnson is their most vocal adherent. "In our opinion it's senseless to make a tree look like a dog or canary – something which it is not; it makes sense to help the tree bring out the perfect tree within itself and for it to be appreciated for that perfection. We help the tree be the best tree it can be."

Unfortunately, the Green Pyramid movement has never won a prize at the Topiary contest, largely because they have normally finished their shaping after about five minutes and spend the rest of the time in the pub. They then normally heckle the winners at the awards ceremony, which doesn't win them many friends in Northallerton.

Playing Card Festival at Willoughby Waterless

Playing cards have played an important role in people's lives for centuries. The Playing Card Festival has been held annually since 1682 to celebrate all the non-gambling uses that playing cards can be used for.

It all began when the wife of local gambler Ralph Meadows decided that she would remove all gambling temptation from his life. She picked up his pack of cards and threw them individually out of the window. Ralph noticed that some of the cards travelled more than 100 yards and bragged one day in the pub that his wife could throw cards further than anyone else. The challenge was inevitably taken up by his drinking friends and the contest was established, taking place on St George's Day in a farmer's field.

Fifty contestants each took a playing card from the Presiding Judge's pack. The order of throwing was decided by the number of the card (aces high) – in order of importance the suits were hearts, clubs, diamonds, and spades. The first thrower was the two of hearts and the final thrower was the ace of spades. Ralph's wife, Jenny, had the eight of diamonds and hurled it 112 yards seven inches.

She used a flicking motion of her wrist that made the most of her powerful forearms strengthened by years of throwing hay bales into the upper floor of the barn. Since that time the eight of diamonds has been known as the Jenny Strongarm card. Jenny Meadows won the first six throwing contests before an accident when moving an entire haystack left her with a damaged elbow.

Her record distance lasted until 1792 when Jeremiah

Morse, a local boxer, hurled the King of clubs 119 yards. He employed Jenny's flicking motion in his throw but also incorporated the rotation method used by discus throwers to gain momentum.

In 1800 the organizers decided to add an accuracy test to the distance event in a bid to extend the interest of the contest to the more effete members of society. Players use five cards and try to land a card into saucepans set at five different distances from the thrower: seven yards, 14 yards, 28 yards, 35 yards and 50 yards. Each person scores four points for landing the card in the saucepan, two points for getting the card to balance on the rim, and one point if the card rests against the saucepan – touching doesn't count.

Jasper Bartram won the first contest with a score of 12 comprising two direct hits and two cards landing on the rim of the saucepan and remaining there. This is the only time that anyone has balanced two cards on the rim of a saucepan in the same contest. Nora Smith is the only person to have scored a perfect 20 in this contest in consecutive years, performing the feat in 1956 and 1957, using what she called her waterfall technique. This comprises throwing the card high into the air and letting it fall vertically into the saucepan. This technique doesn't work well in high winds and Nora Smith scored zero in 1958 when there was a heavy storm in the vicinity.

Another element added to the contest was the card structure contest, which started in 1869 after the Suez Canal was opened. This element was first held in an organiser's shed because of the need for stillness, but the contest soon outgrew the shed and is now held in the local sports centre.

There are two types of competition – the first starts at 8 a.m. and is the 'Build the Biggest Structure out of Cards" contest, which lasts until 6 p.m. No glue or any additional material can be used to hold the cards together. The largest structure ever made was the Pyramid of Cheops created in

1973 by Sandra Parsons, which had a base of 15 yards on each side and had risen to a height of twelve feet by the time 6 p.m. arrived.

The other construction competition relates to contestants creating a representation of a given building such as the Eiffel Tower, Stonehenge, or the Houses of Parliament. Each person has three hours to construct their version of these famous buildings using just playing cards. The winner will be the person with the most accurate rendition of the building. Reggie Swinson has won this contest five times since 1998. He uses two playing cards for each element of the construction giving his structures extra strength, rigidity, and permanence. Indeed, his model of the Coliseum from 2001 is on show in the local museum, due to the accuracy of the representation. It stands next to the museum's only item of Roman pottery.

All the doors to the building are kept locked throughout the contest; this was after the disaster of 1958 when someone came in through the doors followed by a huge gust of wind that destroyed the structures.

Biscuit Rolling from Barnsley

In the UK there are many contests involving the humble biscuit, ranging from building competitions to throwing events. However, in Barnsley the biscuits are just rolled for fun, so that in the words of the original organizer Rufus Moxon, "the biscuit is conserved in its entirety and can still be consumed – what's the point of breaking a perfectly good biscuit just for fun – what a waste of money that would be."

The contest was started in 1934 and has been going strong since then, even during the time of Margaret Thatcher. The contest takes place on the day of the first full moon after the sixth Sunday after Len Hutton's birthday on June 23rd.

There are many different skills contests. The oldest is the rolling the biscuit through the cricket stumps competition, which takes place at the cricket club. Competitors stand in one popping crease and have to roll their biscuit down the pitch and make sure it passes between the stumps at the other end – each person has three biscuits and whoever succeeds in bisecting the stumps is through to the next round. Wilfrid Hirst has won this contest five times – his advice is as follows: "it's just like bowls – same delivery, same pace, except it's a biscuit you're bowling so you have to have more of a follow through – and don't bounce the thing as it will disintegrate on the pitch." Contestants aren't allowed to replace broken biscuits, which means that people who employ a "bouncing bomb" technique have never won the contest.

There is also a distance event at the local athletics track, which takes place along the home straight. Four people take part in each heat; at the sound of the starter's gun they run to the starting line and release their biscuits. Each biscuit must be in contact with the track at all times after it has been released and must not go outside its lane otherwise it will be disqualified. There's always a gap of one lane between each competitor to reduce the chances of interference by a waywardly thrown digestive. The "Usain Bolt" of the biscuit sprint is Sandra Perkins, who has won the event in five of the last seven years, using digestives that she keeps in the freezer to make them harder. Sandra was a promising sprinter until she heard of the Biscuit Rolling and then her head was turned: "I could run't hundred in 12 seconds, burra never were going to get much better; T' Biscuit Rolling offered me immortality and a plaque in the cricket club en all."

Nowhere in the rules does it say that the biscuit has to be round. Some people have tried using custard creams with rounded edges but the inherent weakness of a modified biscuit eventually causes a fatal disintegration at a critical moment.

The other distance event is the hill roll where people release their biscuit at the top of the hill and hope it rolls down the hill further than anyone else's. The road is closed for the event and all parked cars are removed for the day. People do run after their biscuits and are allowed to remove obstacles from its path such as leaves, dogs and traffic wardens who are scratching their heads wondering where all the cars have gone.

The other accuracy event takes place at the Golf Club, which is used for the entire day. Contestants 'play' the whole 18 holes individually, walking from green to green with a counting judge. At each green there's a pre-determined place where every contestant must roll their biscuit from. The aim is to get their biscuit in the hole in as few rolls as possible and the person with the lowest total of rolls over the 18 holes wins the prize of a set of golf clubs. The lowest total was 37 by Lawrie Percival in 1961 using a Jaffa Cake he called Palmer: "Palmer were a great jaffa; as soon as he came out of the packet I knew he were a champion – the jam content was low and the chocolate was spread thinly – an absolute joy to play with."

Cheese Carving in Wensleydale

Wensleydale is a crumbly white cheese from North Yorkshire. This cheese is difficult to cut without pieces falling onto the ground, which might explain why the cheese cutters of this part of the world are regarded as the finest around. The carvers in the dale held competitions amongst themselves for hundreds of years before allowing anyone else to take part. Characters such as Elias Cattermole, Fred Heathcote, Bert Boycott and Roger Vaughan are the stuff of legend – each able to carve the most intricate animals and birds from the crumbliest cheese in the 60-minute time limit.

In 1831, the big decision was made to extend the contest to people from outside the dale, even from Lancashire, just so long as they carved Wensleydale cheese and didn't bring their own cheese with them. In the 1832 contest Bert Boycott won first prize for carving a falcon plunging upon its prey and local carvers continued to dominate until 1862 when Elsie Jerrard from Arkengarthdale became the first 'outsider' to win for her rendition of a cat curled up in some grass. Elsie's comment upon being announced the winner was "It were abaht time someone else wun't carving – this'll giv them Wensley people a shock."

The contest was further extended in 1900 when outside cheese carving contests were included for the first time, although the Right Grand Prize – the most prestigious award – was only awarded for carving Wensleydale. The outside cheeses added in 1900 were Lancashire, Red Leicester, Double Gloucester, Cheshire and Stilton. All of these cheeses, apart from Stilton, are easier to carve and so more people enter these events.

Contestants can bring their own 'outsider' cheese with

them, but it has to be examined by the Contamination Judge before it can be entered in the contest. This judge will ensure that it hasn't already been carved, even partially, and that there's no substance on the surface of the cheese that will make it easier to carve. This latter check is because of Christopher Ollerenshaw, who in 1903 arrived in Wensleydale with a Red Leicester cheese coated in some glue-like substance, which made carving intricate patterns easier. Ollerenshaw would have won a prize if it weren't for the rule that contestants have to eat all the discarded cheese. Ollerenshaw ate this cheese but was then taken to hospital with severe stomach pains and admitted his attempt at cheating – "one day I spilt wallpaper paste in't kitchen and it went all over't food including cheese – after, when ah cut me cheese I culdn't help but notice that it were harder to cut but none crumbled off, so t'idea were born as it were." Ollerenshaw was banned for life and none of his relations will ever be allowed to compete either.

There are no limits to the size of the cheese being carved, but the rule about eating the discarded crumbs does put off most people from bringing larger pieces of cheese to carve.

In 1973, the UK joined the EEC and the organizers decided to allow people to carve cheeses from the other countries of the EEC including France and Italy. The Camembert contest was particularly messy and no prize was awarded that year as no-one could create a recognizable carving. Indeed no award has ever been given in this category – the nearest there's ever been to success was in 1998 when Jacques Jacquard attempted to carve a Camembert cheese that had been placed in a freezer 48 hours prior to carving time. Jacquard created a beautiful rendition of the Eiffel Tower, but sadly it dissolved into a creamy mess before the judging started. Jacquard accused Elliott Dibble of aiding the reheating process using a hairdryer and there was a brief scuffle. From this time, grooming products and pre-frozen cheeses have been banned from the contest.

Contestants can use any sharp implement to carve, just so long as the item isn't used in a threatening manner towards another contestant or their artistic creation.

In modern times, Stanley Jardine has won the most events at the Cheese Carving contest with 23 victories between 1956 and 2007. Stanley started carving Wensleydale cheese and then broadened his horizons to include Lancashire and Cheshire cheese too. His chosen implement was a six-inch long knife with a sharp pointed end used for defining feathers and fur. Jardine explained his success as follows: "you have to learn on the crumbly cheeses so that your techneek is honed to perfection as quickly as possible – there's nowt worse than carving summat bootiful and then it crumbles to bits with one careless cut at t'end. Learning on t'Wensley helps the concentration too, so that by time tha starts on them southern cheeses such as Lanky Sher then everything's so much easier."

Feather Balancing from Rye

The Feather Balancing contest has been held in Rye every September 7th since 1673 and was originally begun to commemorate the 100th anniversary of the visit of Elizabeth I to the town. The contest was created because of the local fable that one of the Queen's peacock feathers blew off her costume and was picked up by local farmer Walter de Groote, who went down on one knee and returned the feather back to Elizabeth. She remarked how wonderful it was that de Groote could balance the feather on the end of his finger. De Groote replied that he could balance a feather on other parts of his anatomy too "if she wulde like to watche."

De Groote was detained in the Tower of London for 25 years for his impertinence and was lucky to escape with his head. It was rumoured that the ravens kept away from his cell as de Groote would take any opportunity to steal feathers from them to practice his art.

The Confederation of Cinque Ports is a historic series of coastal towns in Kent and Sussex originally formed for military and trade purposes. This confederation comprises five ports: Hastings, New Romney, Hythe, Dover, and Sandwich and two so-called "Antient Towns," Rye and Winchelsea. A royal charter of 1155 established the ports to provide 57 ships for 15 days' service to the king annually.

Entrance to the Feather Balancing contest was confined to representatives of these five ports and two towns until 1973 when the contest went international. Originally there was only one category of feather, peacock, and one method of balancing, on the finger. The first winner was Simon de Vere, who balanced a feather on his finger for seven minutes 26 seconds. Once de Vere was pronounced the winner the contest was over. Organisers quickly realised that a contest should last longer than seven minutes and so came up with more categories for the 1674 contest.

The number of feather categories was increased to five: peacock, sparrow, crow, chicken, and goose. People could balance these feathers on their fingers or noses or could perform 'ye tricks'. There was even a 100-yard race for people who were balancing a feather on their finger.

Ted Corbett was the big winner of 1674, winning the feather on the nose balancing contests for all feathers apart from the chicken one, which was won by Brian Moult in a time of 23 minutes and 18 seconds. There was controversy in the sparrow feather balancing on the finger contest when the winner Barry Piggott was accused of cheating by Jem Mace, who claimed that Piggott was using glue to help the balancing. Upon close inspection it was found that Mace was correct and Piggott was banned *sine die.* From this time each contestant has to shake hands with the Shaking Judge before starting to balance his feather – if any foreign substance is found then the contestant is banned for 10 years.

There was also a problem in the 100-yard race when Albert Smythe was found to have carved his sparrow feather so that it sat more snugly over his finger. He was banned for life and a new rule was introduced: "due to carvinge, whitlingge, altering, and cheeting of highest order, from this daye forthe ye 100-yarde race will only involve ye folkes who have no connexion to there feather." What this means is that people are allocated a feather by the Handing Out Judge at the start of the race.

The tricks contest of 1674 was won by the astonishing Oliver Allan, who even to this day holds the record for the number of tricks victories at 46. Allan was able to balance a feather on his finger, throw it lightly into the air so that it landed on his nose, and from there cajole it onto his elbow and then down his arm to his finger.

The other record holders are Roger Byrom, who won 76 feather balancing on the finger contests between 1816 and 1852, including two years 1832 and 1845 when he won all five. Elspeth Hodgkins won 63 feather balancing on the nose contests between 1876 and 1901. Hodgkins admitted that she had a big nose and might have been drowned in former times as a witch, but she didn't think it was all down to her mighty snout: "the most important thingge is to practice and have good balance; watch the feather at all times and respond to its gyrations with slow deliberate movements. Never panic and never sneeze as your chances will disappear." This is good advice as Hodgkins' time in the 1891 Sparrow feather balancing on the nose contest of four hours and 23 minutes is still a record.

The 100-yard race record is 32 seconds in 1767 by Derek Boyle using a peacock feather. He explained his success as follows: "Aye were given a shortish fether with a sharpp pointe and I thought to meself, Derek, I thought, this here fether will fall off unless ye hold yer finger at an anggle so I did and I was able to walk quitte quickish and won."

Duck Quacking Festival in Cirencester

When hunting a duck it's a real advantage to be able to sound like a duck rather than a human being carrying a gun. This advantage will allow you to get closer to the bird before giving it both barrels with your shotgun.

This was the rationale behind the duck imitators of Cirencester, who held contests in the 14th and 15th centuries to select the best duck impersonator. As time progressed the impersonations became more important than the shooting as personal pride became involved at the expense of blood lust.

Eventually, interest in imitating other animals began to grow; not only ducks could be heard in the pub but also cows, horses, cats, and badgers. This was disconcerting to the other customers and also convinced the local squire Rupert de Courtney the people of Cirencester had an unparalleled gift for duck imitation that wasn't being channelled in the right direction. In 1726 he decided to hold a contest, open to all, to decide who could best imitate a duck.

De Courtney decided to hold the contest on October 4th, the feast day of St Francis of Assisi, who is the patron saint of animals. The contest attracted people from across the Cotswolds. There were 132 entrants and lots were drawn to decide the order of the participants. De Courtney had decided that the best judge of whether the duck impersonations were accurate would be a real duck.

It just so happened that a local family had adopted a duck called Jessica. She was placed on a table in her own nest and her reactions to each impersonator were watched closely – the more interested in the impersonator Jessica became the more marks were awarded by the human observers.

After 78 impersonators had tried to interest Jessica by shouting "Quack, quack, quack" at the top of their voices, she was almost falling asleep because of boredom. However, competitor 79, Samuel John, then gave his impersonation and Jessica stood bolt upright and flew away. The observers decided that scaring the judge was against the rules and John was banned for five years "to give him time to practice a better duck impersonation."

When Jessica was found and had calmed down sufficiently, the other 53 impersonators were allowed to make their attempts. As nobody had even stirred Jessica previously, Dave Simmons thought that getting any reaction from the duck might win him the contest, so when it was his turn, at number 113, he shouted "Woof, woof, woof." Jessica looked up, flew directly at Simmons, and pecked him viciously on the nose, before returning to her nest. Simmons was led away with blood pouring from his face. To add to his discomfort he was banned for life for contravening the spirit of the contest. Since that time, the number 113 has been called "The Curse of the Duck Impersonators," and people given this number have never done very well.

Eventually contestant number 126, Brenda Spooner, stirred Jessica's interest by trilling "Quick, quock, quack" and then clucking and moving her arms around like a chicken. Jessica watched her intently and then quacked back. This was enough for Spooner to be awarded the contest with a winning score of one – everyone else apart from John and Simmons scored zero.

Brenda Spooner went on to win the contest a further six times in a row and increased her score each year, culminating with a 14 in 1732, when Jessica responded with unadulterated bliss to Spooner's impersonations, followed her out of the tent, and refused to return. This led to a new rule whereby the previous year's winner always goes last in the contest.

To this day Jessica's descendants judge the contest. The latest judge is Desmond the duck, who has been presiding duck since 2007 and is very hard to please. The highest score during Desmond's time has been three in 2009 when Wayne Windsor was the winner. Windsor's previous winning score had been 15 in 2003 when Patrick the duck was judging.

There haven't been many injuries throughout the contest's history. The worst was in 1962 when Roger Parfitt became so exasperated with the lack of effect his impersonation was having on Sylvia the duck that he started shouting "orange sauce you stupid duck." Sylvia walked across and fixed Parfitt with a steely glare – she then flew at his groin and as he protected himself switched her attack to his ears and eyes causing several lacerations. Parfitt was taken to hospital where he had to have a tetanus jab and was then told he had been banned from the contest for 15 years for judging abuse.